Praise for Daniel Black's *Don't Cry for Me*

"*Don't Cry for Me* is a perfect song. At turns intense and funny, tender and brutally honest, Jacob's letter to his son, Isaac, is revelatory. While the story is an unflinching account of a family and a community in the Black American Midwest coming of age in the modern now, it is also full of that which makes us all human: full of fathers trying to understand sons, sons trying to understand fathers, parents feeling as if they have failed children, children realizing how they have passed their own traumas on to others and so on. It's a beautiful book. Read it."

—Jesmyn Ward

"Black manages to capture, and really free characters, scenes, and so much subtext we've felt, but rarely seen or heard in American literature. The book is unafraid of the pungent slivers of joy and those dazzling shards of horror that accompany loneliness and progress. *Don't Cry for Me* is literally the book my favorite books needed to read. It is an unparalleled literary achievement that already feels like it will, of all things, endure."

—Kiese Laymon, author of *Heavy: An American Memoir*

"*Don't Cry for Me* marries soliloquy to epistolary for a sustained view of a man's change of mind. From boyhood to his final days, we follow Jacob Swinton, and in so doing, we gain a lesson in a rural Black history yet taught in school. But beyond this book's formal dexterity and particularized view of changing times, is its attention to the idea of family, its hope that blood ties us without chaining us."

—Jericho Brown, Pulitzer Prize–winning poet of *The Tradition*

"A panorama of a family where the history and the future combine through the impactful storytelling of a gifted writer."

—Ravi Howard, author of *Like Trees, Walking*

"A beautiful, thoughtful novel about living and dying."

—Dana Williams, Howard University professor of African American literature and chair, Department of English

"A book that is so dearly needed and has been for generations. For anyone who cares about Black men, gender, sexuality, and healing, this book is a balm that helps connect the dots between legacies of oppression and opportunities to change course. Do yourself and future generations a favor by reading this beautiful literary work."

—R. L'Heureux Lewis-McCoy, author of *Inequality in the Promised Land: Race, Resources, and Suburban Schooling*

ALSO BY DANIEL BLACK

DON'T CRY FOR ME

A NOVEL

DANIEL BLACK

HANOVER
SQUARE
PRESS

HANOVER
SQUARE
PRESS™

Recycling programs
for this product may
not exist in your area.

ISBN-13: 978-1-335-42573-7

Don't Cry for Me

Copyright © 2022 by Daniel Black

This edition published by arrangement with Harlequin Books S.A.

Hanover Square Press
22 Adelaide St. West, 41st Floor
Toronto, Ontario M5H 4E3, Canada
HanoverSqPress.com
BookClubbish.com

Printed in U.S.A.

To Ernest J. Gaines,
who started the public healing of black fathers and sons years ago

DON'T CRY FOR ME

AUTHOR NOTE

When, in 2013, my father was diagnosed with Alzheimer's, I knew what it meant—he'd soon forget what he'd done or said to me over the years. In fact, he'd need my sympathy, perhaps my financial assistance, as his memory faded away. For a long time, I had wanted us to hash things out, to speak honestly about how we had hurt or disappointed one another over the years. But Daddy's mind left like a dream at dawn. And now the encounter could happen only in my imagination.

So that was where I went. I saw, in my mind, my father leaning over a legal pad, writing, as best he could, something very private, very painful that couldn't wait another day. I imagined him ancestral, though still in the flesh, such that he knew and understood everything about me. And I imagined him unashamed. I wondered what he'd say if he could stare into my heart. This book is his response, his desperate plea.

My father grew up in a time when black children meant

nothing to America. Most of them, including him, didn't have a birth certificate. Their care, their education, their self-worth was optional. Whether they lived or died was insignificant to the state. For the most part, their existence centered around work and church. And even the church taught them that they were "wretches" and "sinners undone," black children of Ham who, without a forgiving God, had no hope in this life or the next. Children of my father's generation were taught that dreams were a waste of time. Schooling happened only when there was no labor to be done, and that wasn't very often.

This is the world that shaped my father's consciousness. In his old age, he retired from his job as a mechanic, and the state informed him that he needed a birth certificate in order to draw social security. He told them he never had one. They responded, "Get a birth certificate form and make it up. If you don't know your birthday, just choose a day." I was horrified at the arbitrary nature of his life. Only then did I understand his harsh, insensitive demeanor. In some ways, he envied the life he had provided for his children. He, too, had wanted knowledge, travel, enlightenment, but such was laughable for a dark black boy in the 1940s. So he hoped for me. Yet my freedom angered him. It made me question his world, his convictions, his God. After college, I wanted nothing to do with his idea of manhood. He wanted no parts of my fluidity. We were never united in our hearts again.

Yet once Alzheimer's took Daddy's mind and softened his boldness, I discovered a man who was more than a field plow. He wanted what I wanted—to mean something to the world, to make a difference in someone's life, to be admired for the man he was. But we never achieved that mutual clarity. So this book, this record of a poor black father's appeal, is what any dying daddy might say to his son. More than anything, I want readers to reconsider the capacity of our fathers' hearts. Many of them were handed so little, yet we expected so much. They gave more than they had, but less than we needed. They were burdened with a notion of manhood that destroyed so many sons' lives; but they didn't know another notion to teach. In the end, many destroyed themselves, too.

If they'd been allowed to dream, they might've expected sons who were not carbon copies of themselves. They might've imagined boys in all their glory, dancing before the world without shame. They might've granted a queer son permission and affirmation to be himself—regardless of the world's reaction. They might've known that some spirits come into the world to disrupt normalcy and thereby create space for the despised and rejected. And they might've understood, finally, that every son is an eternal blessing.

If they'd been allowed to dream.

NOVEMBER 12TH, 2003

Dear Isaac,

For a life like mine, there is no redemption. I wish I was old. Dying ain't so bad if a man is old, but when he's my age—sixty-two—it's a sad and pitiful thing. If I was eighty, I could die in peace. Eighty's a good dying age. But a man in his sixties should still have his strength, his good senses. My strength is practically spent. Every day, cancer consumes a little more of it, leaving me to wonder when it'll run out altogether. My mind, however, is still with me, so I should say some things while I can.

It's been…what? Ten, fifteen years or better? After your mother died, days passed into years.

I'm not long for this world. My days of grace are far spent. At the end of a life, memories are clouded. But perhaps with what I'm about to say, you will know why I did what I did. Whether you forgive me or not will be up to you.

★ ★ ★

You should know that, during the years between us, I became a reader. I know this sounds funny, since you never saw me with a book, but in my darkest hour, your mother encouraged me to give it a try and, finally, for once, I followed her. I was horrible at first, mispronouncing words and skipping ideas I couldn't understand, but after a while I got the hang of it and became pretty good. Reading was something I could do alone, so I stuck with it.

I'm still in the house, our house, where everything happened. Not much has changed. The brown velvet sofa, worn and ragged, still sits against the wall like an invalid staring into nothing. The console TV went out years ago, but I never got rid of it. Instead, I put a flat-screen on top of it. It looks funny, really, this shiny new thing sitting piggyback on an ancient thing, but with no one to impress, I rarely think about it. Your mother's high-back chair, where she sat many evenings reading *Ebony* magazines or romance novels, rests where it always did, opposite the sofa, facing the living room door. I imagine her there sometimes, thumbing pages and nodding or frowning or laughing out loud.

Most memorable perhaps is the little oval kitchen table where we shared most of our meals. It reminds me of her and you and us. I don't eat there. I take my meals in the living room, something I would never have done when you were a kid. But most days I'm good to eat at all. Cancer strips one's appetite and energy so completely. Yet every now and then I can swallow a few morsels, enough to live another day and finish writing what I want to say to you.

★ ★ ★

Let me start with this: love wasn't a requirement of men in my day. It wasn't a man's achievement. In the sixties, when you were born, love was a woman's passion, a mother's hope. Fathers had far different obsessions: food, shelter, clothing, protection. My job was to assure you had these things, and I did that.

Truth is, the world changed faster than I could. When I was a boy, we knew what a boy was. There were signs—agreed upon signs—that left no one confused or unsure. Girls had certain features; boys had others. It was simple as that. Yet you came along and muddied my clarity. You loved hugs and kisses; you wept at the beauty of things; you frowned at trucks and baseball gloves. But you were a boy. *My* boy. And I meant to correct whatever had gone wrong in you.

I need to start at the beginning if you are to understand everything. Yet the beginning isn't *your* beginning. Or even mine. It's ours.

Slavery did a number on black people. We haven't survived it yet. The institution is over, but its aftereffects still linger. We try not to think about it, our time in bondage, but it shapes who we are. I'm convinced of this. We worked for free for four hundred years while our self-worth went down the drain. We learned to despise ourselves—not white folks—because our failure, we think, was having been captured at all. And we know that some of our own people participated. We know that. We've never forgiven them either. Perhaps that's why some of us hate us. When they look in the mirror, all they see is contempt for someone unforgivable.

I can't remember when it started, but, as a little boy, I recall wanting to be someone else. Granddaddy used to comb my hair like he was mad at it. *This some wooly shit, boy! You sho got some nappy-ass hair*, he'd mumble until he tamed the wild bush or cut it off altogether. I remember seeing white boys in town and watching their hair wave easily in the wind, and I wondered why God hadn't given me that. A few Colored boys had soft curly hair, but they were light skinned. We were dark. Black dark. *All Nigga*, Granddaddy liked to say.

Because of this, we lived lives of desperate hope, afraid that white people's disapproval equaled our destruction. Everything we did, whether we were aware or not, we did with white people in mind. Our life's aim was to make them believe we had value and worth, so we spent our nights trying to figure out what they liked, then spent our days trying to do it. We still haven't pleased them, and truth is, we never will.

You'll think I'm crazy, but I met Death several months ago. I didn't see her, but I sensed her. I felt something brush my arm, like a cool breeze, and saw my whole life flash before me. When people say this, it is true. Everyone I ever loved I saw in my mind, and I knew it was time to say goodbye. But Death didn't rush me. She lingered there, with the scent of sweet perfume and pork-seasoned collard greens. I liked that aroma. It reminded me of Grandma on Sunday afternoons. Anyway, I told Death, "Just give me a minute. I'm writing something important to my son." Her fragrance waned, so I believed she'd granted my request. Perhaps this was all in my mind, but it felt real to me. I didn't fear her. I told her I would be ready soon—if she would let me finish what I had begun.

NOVEMBER 13TH, 2003

I was born a slave, Isaac—almost literally. My grandfather raised me, and his father had been a slave until age eighteen. That's long enough to shape one's way of thinking and pass it along for generations. Even after freedom, we were not free. We were lynched and beaten and mobbed and raped and burned out and stolen from and cheated and denied and degraded and humiliated and insulted and belittled and disrespected so much that we believed white folks were God's chosen people. They had everything we wanted, it seemed. Even poor whites. At least they could go to town and be served. We had to watch our backs everywhere we went. We were never safe in this country. Can you imagine that? A life where you and your family are *never* safe? Sunrise is a torture because you never sleep. Not that deep, snoring kind of sleep. People died young back then—forty and fifty— because, as the expression goes, *there was no rest for the weary.*

And we were the weary. We were field hands, tillers of the soil, whose mirror image was the dirt itself. We took pride in working because it's what we knew, what we did best. We never believed we meant much. I see that now. We even buried one another without tombstones. No need remembering one whose only achievement was a decent spring crop or a house full of hungry children. Save that money and repair the roof. That's how folks thought back then. That's how we'd been taught to think.

We loved each other—if love is respect. Yet respect wasn't what you and your generation wanted. You wanted something you could feel in your heart, and I didn't know what that was. My generation had never had it. Granddaddy or Grandma never kissed me or read to me or touched me lovingly. I don't think Granddaddy could read at all, although Grandma could a little. The only time Granddaddy touched me was to whoop me, and I mean he whooped hard. A whoopin is different from a spanking. A spanking happens on your behind; a whoopin happens all over you. And when Granddaddy got through with you, you'd have to get somewhere and sit down. But he loved me. I understand that now. His behavior was simply the way of black parenting. Every child I knew was beaten senseless. Elders were callous and unfeeling, as if afraid to love us. Slavery had left them that way.

Granddaddy was worst of all. Nothing moved his cool, dry countenance. I rarely saw him laugh and never saw him cry. He approached life as a test of endurance, so each day he handled chores and disappointments as if trying to show God he was unbreakable. But his breaking point would come.

★ ★ ★

My favorite person in the world was my brother, Esau. I cannot tell you the way I loved him. He was a year and a half older than me, and he was my hero.

Growing up in Arkansas, we used to lie in bed together, whispering about things. Well, I'd whisper while Esau listened. He wasn't much of a talker, but he seemed to enjoy hearing me, so I always had something to say.

"Where do stars come from?" I asked one rainy night.

I knew he wasn't asleep. When he slept, he made a soft, grumbling sound, like an old electric fan.

Suddenly, he turned toward me, rubbed my course, kinky hair, and said, "They're God's thoughts."

"God's thoughts? Wow. He's got a lotta thoughts."

Esau chuckled quietly.

"What do you think God thinks about?"

"I don't know," he whispered, shaking his head. "Probably us."

"Us? You think God knows us? Out of alllllllll the people in the world?"

"God knows everybody, Isaac. And everything."

I loved how Esau rubbed my head. His heavy hand massaged my scalp sensually, like a loving God might do.

"God knows what I think?"

"Yep."

"And what you think?"

"Yep."

"And what Granddaddy and Grandma think?"

"Yes, boy."

I heard Esau's slight irritation, so I hushed and let his hand nurture me. Then I asked, "What do you think about?"

At first he didn't answer, but then he mumbled, "Mom. Dad."

His voice trembled. I didn't want him to cry because I would've cried, so I tried to change the subject, but Granddaddy yelped from the other room, "You boys take yo ass to sleep, hear me? Don't make me come in there after you."

That ended our talking, but Esau rubbed my head until I went to sleep. The older we got, the less he did it, and the day he stopped altogether, my joy disappeared.

NOVEMBER 14TH, 2003

Today is a bad day. I'm sick as a dog, but I'm trying to write anyway. I don't want to run out of time before I finish, so I'm pressing on with what little strength I have.

Back in the country, we never had electricity. Just coal oil lamps and an icebox. Not a refrigerator but a literal icebox in which a block of ice cooled churned butter and eggs. Everything else we canned or smoked. Food was better back then, but it was hard to come by. And because we had very little money, we had to grow our own. We made two dollars a day pickin cotton, and, as children, we never got the money. Granddaddy got ours and did with it whatever needed to be done.

One year he saved enough for an operation. He had a pain in his side that couldn't be ignored. I recall a doctor coming to our house and telling Granddaddy to get the operation or the undertaker. If it wasn't for your uncle Esau and me, he would've chosen the undertaker.

The doctor brought his instruments to the house and sterilized them with boiling water and bourbon. Granddaddy refused a hospital room but submitted to the procedure in his own bed. There was no anesthesia back then—not for poor black folks. Grandma put Esau and me outdoors when everything began. Said she didn't want us upset by Granddaddy's screaming. But Granddaddy never murmured a sound. Just one soft grunt, the doctor said, when he reached inside him and pulled out his appendix. Other than that, he stared at the ceiling as if daydreaming. When the doctor finished, he told Grandma to make the old man rest a week. Said the recuperation was critical to his fullest healing. She nodded but knew better. When we reentered the house, she made us sit in absolute silence as the sun went down. Granddaddy slept like a dead man.

Next morning, he dragged himself to the breakfast table. Esau and I shuddered; Grandma exploded.

"You can't be up, man! Doctor said you gotta stay in bed the rest of the week. Take yo butt back in there and lay down!"

Granddaddy didn't move. He blinked a few times and asked, "Is we havin breakfast or not?"

"I ain't cookin nothin till you get back in that room!"

"Then I'll cook it myself."

He rose slowly, clearly in pain, till Grandma conceded. "You bout the hardest-headed man alive, Abraham Swinton! Don't know why I fool with you! You ain't got no sense!" and on and on till eventually she hushed her fussing and put breakfast on the table. No one looked at Granddaddy during the meal. We kept our eyes on our own plates, wondering who in the world gets up the morning after an operation like that, prepared to go to the field.

"You ain't doin no plowin today, man!" Grandma insisted. "And I mean it! I'll fight you if I have to. Don't intend to bury you this evenin." He must've taken her seriously. We repaired fences instead.

NOVEMBER 16TH, 2003

Feeling much better today. It's cool and rainy, but every day's a blessing in my condition. Yesterday, the doctor increased my paclitaxel-cisplatin, so I feel better than I have in a long while.

I started school at age six, although I didn't go regularly. It was 1947. Education was a luxury most poor Negro kids in Arkansas couldn't afford. Not monetarily, but timewise. Only when it rained, and it had to rain hard, were we guaranteed a few consistent days. One or two kids went all the time, but not most of us. We were always behind, always missing home-work and failing tests. Miss Ima Briars, our teacher, had the nerve to scold us! We would've done better if we could've. We had to work: picking cotton, chopping beans, cutting wood, hauling hay, plowing fields... You name it. It had to be done. Knowledge could wait—or so our people thought. We had the mindset of ignorance. We simply didn't know any better. We weren't unintelligent; we were just desperate to survive. We thought eating every day was a big deal, and many times it was. Without money or most other resources, black families did what they had to do to keep food on the table.

By ten, I had learned to read, but just barely. Esau never learned. He wasn't good in his books, but he was great with his hands. Granddaddy looked at him with an approving sort of gaze. I envied that. He didn't look at me that way. Even now I wish for it, and Granddaddy is long gone. But my point is about education—or the scarcity of it. We owned no books except a Bible. Granddaddy had his own—*his* Bible—which we weren't allowed to touch. He thumbed it most nights, but certainly didn't read it. Perhaps simply holding it revealed what *thus saith the Lord*. I don't know. I heard about other books but saw only the ones the white school threw away to us. Most were filled with racist bullshit that did us no good. Miss Ima talked of famous white people like Shakespeare and Henry Wadsworth Longfellow. I remember those names because they sounded funny to me. The only black writer she ever mentioned was Paul Laurence Dunbar, but we never read his work. At least not the few days I attended. Truth was, we needed basic 'rithmetic and writing, just enough to get by, and that's what we learned.

Esau only went a year. He could spell his name, but that was about it. And since Granddaddy couldn't imagine what he'd do with more knowledge, he let him stay home and work. But Grandma insisted I go. "Somebody in this family gotta get some learnin," she said. "Cain't all be ignorant." So I was the chosen one. This was no compliment, mind you. I had to do homework *after* we did field work. Yet believing that education would give me a better life, Grandma urged me on. She was right. The ability to read, even a little, would later save my life.

After fourth or fifth grade, my schooling is a blur. I never did well because I missed too many days. I was smart though. Miss Ima said so. She said I could really be somebody—those were her words—if I came more often, but that never happened. I probably went once or twice a month. More in the winter, less in the spring. After eighth grade, I stopped altogether. "That's enough," Granddaddy said casually one evening. "Too much learnin make the boy lazy." Grandma protested. She wanted a high school graduate, but Granddaddy wouldn't have it. "This boy gotta learn how to work better, woman. Readin ain't gon feed him."

"It can!" she declared, but Granddaddy had dropped the matter, which meant it was closed. I never went to school again.

Sometimes on Sunday afternoons, I'd pass the old schoolhouse and recall Miss Ima teaching times tables or reading passages from her favorite books. She'd shout as if preaching, as though her emphasis made her instruction divine. Sometimes she'd quiz us aloud on various topics, and if we didn't know the answer, we'd be in trouble. We sat perfectly upright, our hands clasped and resting on our desks, praying to know whatever Miss Ima might ask. She was a little woman, but she didn't play when it came to education:

"What is fourteen take away nine?"

We'd say, in chorus, "Five!"

"And what is five times six?"

"Thirty!"

"And what is thirty times eleven?"

Some of us would hesitate at this level, but our silence only inflamed her fury: "I said, what is thirty times eleven!"

A smart child, usually one of the Cox kids since they went to school regularly, would say, "Three hundred and thirty!"

At first, I thought I'd be glad to be relieved of homework, but when, over time, friends knew more than me, I longed to return to my place in the fourth row, seventh seat. We sat in alphabetical order, which, for me, always meant I was near the back. Only two people sat behind me: Louise Thompson and Bobby Joe Watkins. He was one of my cut-up buddies, so Miss Ima watched us closely.

The few times I gave a correct answer and Miss Ima praised me still replay in my mind. One day, she thought we were cackling, which we were, and that made her believe we weren't paying attention, so she called me to the board. Why she didn't call him I don't know. My classmates held their breath. I moved forward quickly and stood beside her large wooden desk.

Miss Ima couldn't have been more than five feet two, in heels, and a hundred pounds, but that meant nothing. Her authority, her command of language, her thunderous voice intimidated everyone though most of us could probably have lifted her with one hand.

Ready to rebuke, she'd lean her head back and rest tiny fists upon her narrow waist. She was small, but not fragile. Elegant like crystal glass, but tough as nails.

"Tell me," she began loudly, "what I said is the capital of the country of Russia." She looked away in disgust.

"Moscow," I said confidently, staring at my peers. Their eyes bulged. A few even clapped excitedly.

"Silence! This is not a game, young people!"

Their heads bowed as if in collective prayer. She tried again: "And what did I say are the seven continents of the world?"

Children's heads lifted with great anticipation.

"Um… Africa. Europe. Asia. North America. South America. Australia. And…um…"

Miss Ima stared at me as if hoping I didn't know. But I did.

"Ant-ar-tica."

Applause and cheers burst forth all over the room as children leapt with pride and relief. Miss Ima didn't stop them this time. She nodded and smiled a bit, if I remember correctly, and said to me, amidst the noise, "You just might be somebody one day, Jacob Swinton." I strutted back to my seat, slapping five against every black palm in the room.

Later that day, we were released to recess. Everyone started shouting my name.

"We get Jacob!"

"No, we get Jacob! Y'all had him last time!"

There were always two teams when we played ball, and Bobby Joe and I were always the captains. We were both fast, but I could throw a baseball harder than him, so I was always first to be chosen.

That particular day, Bobby Joe had eight boys on his team, and I had seven boys and one girl. Her name was Francine Fletcher. She was tougher than any boy around, and we all knew it. We'd tried, at various points, to whip or outrun her, and we never won. Not one of us. She was stout as a tree trunk, but not fat. And sweet as could be, with a squeaky little voice. No other girls played with the boys but her. The others played jacks, jump rope, hopscotch, hide-and-seek, and all kinds of hand games. But not Francine. She wanted to play with the boys, she'd said, because boys had more fun. She wasn't fast, but she could slug a baseball deep into the field, so I was happy she was on our team that day.

I messed around with Francine a few times. She did what no black girl was supposed to do, and I liked it. She was never my girlfriend because she wasn't pretty enough, but we enjoyed touching each other. We never went all the way. We just explored each other's bodies the way kids do. I never told anyone, and I guess she didn't either.

Whenever we played ball at school, we chose team names to make the event official. This time, we were the Blackwell Cougars, they were the Blackwell All-stars. The score remained pretty even until Bobby Joe hit a home run with the bases loaded. The All-stars cheered so loudly other girls quit their games and gathered to watch us. Everything, now, was at stake. The score was All-stars 7, Cougars 4. Their last batter hit a fly ball. I caught it, which sent us home to bat. We put Francine up first because she could always get on base. And she did. Girls screamed for her louder than for us.

The next batter, a boy we called Shorty, hit a grounder into left field, allowing Francine to get to second. They asked me to bat next and bring everyone home, which would leave the game tied at seven. Instead, I insisted that someone else bat and load the bases, then I'd bring everyone home for a victory. It was risky, I knew, but I meant to show Bobby Joe and everyone else who was king of the baseball diamond. So we put another batter up who sent a pop-up to right field and got out. Two outs, and two on base. "Just bat, Jacob! Come on!" my teammates whispered with fear. But I refused. I didn't want to tie; I wanted to win. So I convinced them to let another boy bat and we did. He drove a hard ball straight into right field and loaded the bases. The opposing team tried throwing to third, hoping to stop Francine, but they failed, and once again girls screamed her name. She never cracked a smile or waved back. She meant to be taken seriously, and she was.

Miss Ima rang the two-minute warning bell. Everyone froze. Then, my teammates shouted, "Come on, Jacob! You can do this!"

"No pop-ups!"

"Knock it outta sight!"

"Bring 'em all home!"

I stepped forward and swung the bat a few times to loosen my nerves and find my rhythm. The other team backed away in anticipation of a long fly ball. The first throw was a strike, but I missed it.

"Take your time, Jacob!"

"Keep your eye on the ball!"

"Don't let 'em scare you!"

I hit the next ball, but it was a foul, which of course meant strike two. My hands were trembling; I could feel it in the bat. I squeezed harder, trying desperately to steady myself and do what the Cougars needed me to do.

The next throw was too high. I huffed and took a few more practice swings as the catcher retrieved the ball and returned it to the pitcher. Then I planted my feet shoulder-width apart and raised the bat to my right ear. When the pitcher threw this time, I watched the ball like a hawk until it approached the mound. Then I leaned my total strength into the swing and heard the *crack!* as the bat sent the ball into the air. It rose and rose and rose, like a rocket soaring into the sky. I dashed toward first base as the others ran home. The All-stars watched the ball disappear above the trees behind the schoolhouse as Bobby Joe went after it. When I crossed home plate, I was tackled to the ground.

"You did it, Jacob! You did it!"

"Man, you socked that out of sight!"

"The Cougars are the champions!"

And on and on until Miss Ima rang the final bell. Continuing to rumble with excitement, we stomped into the schoolhouse and fell into our respective seats.

"Settle down, children! Settle down!" she called, but our joy bubbled over. She granted us a few seconds, then stared at the class silently. We knew what that meant, so we quieted quickly and huffed until our breathing eased.

"Where is Bobby Joe?" she asked.

We looked around with honest confusion. Someone said, "He ran into the woods after the baseball." Minutes later, he dragged himself into the room, drunk with defeat. Everyone stared, wondering what exactly he'd been doing, but he simply slumped into his seat and rested his head on the desktop. Miss Ima promised to deal with him later.

After school, I caught up with him and asked what happened. He said, "I looked for that ball but couldn't find it."

I bent over with laughter. "What do you mean you couldn't find it?"

"I mean it's not there!"

I roared even louder. In my mind, something magical had happened. I convinced myself that I had knocked that ball clean into eternity. That's right—straight into the afterlife. That's what I told Bobby Joe. He asked if I was crazy, and I said, "You didn't find it, did you?" So we searched those woods after school, both of us intent to prove a point, but there was no ball. He kept glancing at me to see if I was serious, and I kept winking to prove that I was. We hooted and hollered about that till we were grown.

This was boyhood in my day. We built reputations of strength and speed, hard work and resilience, that made our people proud. Girls loved us; lazy boys feared us. I'd dreamed of raising a boy, teaching him everything I knew, training him to be like me.

NOVEMBER 17TH, 2003

I wore myself out yesterday, writing to you, but I slept pretty good last night, so I'm picking up where I left off. These good days won't last long. Cancer is never that kind.

After I quit school, I tried to read on my own, but I was no good at it. Months later, I longed to return, but it was too late. When I picked up a book again, you were a grown man.

One incident, however, at the edge of the playground, lingers in my mind. It happened a few weeks before I left school altogether. I was eleven or twelve, I think. I never told you about it because I was too ashamed. Still am. But if I'm gon tell the truth, I'm gon tell it all.

His name was Strong—Elliott Strong. He was a quiet, shy child who didn't say much, and that was the problem. He spoke softly, as if afraid of being heard, and blinked long curly lashes that looked too feminine for a boy. He was thin, too, almost puny, which certainly didn't help, and, worst of all, he had what we called *good hair*, which meant soft, wavy loops—not hard, kinky coils like the rest of us. We boys envied him because girls adored him. He loved their presence, their constant attention, their kind, sweet demeanor, and we thought it our job to toughen him up.

Elliott sat on a large tree stump, minding his own business, twiddling a blade of grass. A group of boys and I approached and asked if he was a sissy. He began to cry, which fueled our rage. Large tears rolled down his pronounced cheekbones. We repeated the question and he shook his head and turned away, but we wouldn't back down. We teased him and slapped him about pretty good. Miss Ima was inside, marking exams, so she never saw us. Teachers didn't spend time on the playground back then. Children didn't need supervision simply to play. Or so it seemed. Anyway, Elliott wouldn't fight back, inviting us to do with him as we pleased. I had absolutely no sympathy for him. He was a punk, a weakling who needed to learn to stand up for himself, so I supported the cause.

The ruckus elevated until we formed a circle around Elliott and exposed ourselves to him. He closed his eyes and trembled, but that didn't save him. All the boys, except Bobby Joe and me, made Elliott suck them. The only reason we didn't participate is because we feared our granddaddies' wrath. Throughout our childhood, Bobby Joe and I compared welts across our bodies and argued about whose granddaddy beat the hardest. Still, we stood there and watched. We hated that Elliott was so gullible, so easily submissive. We kicked and cursed him, Bobby Joe and me, while the rest of them did that nasty thing. I believed those other boys were worse than us, but of course they weren't. All of us destroyed him that day. And we did it happily—without shame or remorse. I've told myself, over the years, that we didn't know any better. We were taught *what* to think—not *how*. There is a difference, you know. It never crossed our minds that we were destroying someone's life.

The worst part is that, after the circle dissolved and we reentered the school, boys giggled and snickered as if something funny had occurred. Miss Ima reprimanded us several times. She saw Elliott's grief and asked about the matter, but he shook his head and remained silent. He spent the afternoon smearing tears across his cheeks, trying not to crumble. His emotional distress only humored us further. Miss Ima asked me after school what happened on the playground, but I lied and said I didn't know. We walked home together, those rowdy boys and I, as they retold the story of Elliott giving them pleasure. They said he wanted it, yearned for it, sucked like it was sweet. We screamed with delight.

Yet, by morning, Elliott was dead.

Everyone whispered about it at school the next day. It rained so badly we had to stay inside. I remember it well. Girls cried silently while boys sat about with folded arms and downcast eyes. No one claimed to know anything. We boys remained tight-lipped. We never knew if perhaps one of us had feared that Elliott might tell, so he did some unforgivable thing to stop him, or if Elliott believed what we thought about him and took his own life. We simply stumbled about, numb and silent, not wanting anyone to ask us about the previous day's events. A few girls frowned at us, knowing that something had happened, but since they didn't know what, they couldn't accuse us. They knew we'd never tell, and we never did.

His family, all fifteen of them, was devastated. Granddaddy and I went by when he heard the news. I didn't want to go, but my refusal would've been suspicious, so I surrendered and went. When we stepped into the Strongs' living room, I saw gloom, hanging in the air like a gray cloud. At first I thought it was smoke, but I didn't smell anything, and it was far too warm for a fire anyway. Everyone's head was bowed, as if in constant prayer, and when Mr. Strong stood to shake Granddaddy's hand, he barely mumbled his appreciation for our coming. I knew a few of the younger siblings, but I didn't say anything to them. I just stood next to Granddaddy like his shadow, moving whenever he moved, until we left. There was a sadness in that house I can't explain. Again I saw it—thick and gray in the air, just above my head. When we stepped outside, Granddaddy said, "Worse thang in the world a man can do, boy, is lose his son." He shook his head all the way home.

I heard later that Elliott's school-age siblings didn't return until long after the burial. There was no funeral; I don't know why. Just whisperings of something bad that happened for reasons no one could explain. Only we boys knew what we'd done. I couldn't believe Elliott had died because of us. Yes, we'd been wrong, but was it enough to kill him? Truth was, we believed the real infraction to be Elliott's weakness. He'd done what no boy should ever do. He should've at least fought, and we might've respected him, but all he did was cry and submit to what we demanded. We hated him for that, so we degraded him, hoping he'd rebel and become strong like the rest of us.

He didn't.

NOVEMBER 19TH, 2003

I can't believe I told you about Elliott. I swore never to tell anyone that terrible story. But telling it is the only way I know to honor him. This means his life is no longer a secret. That *is* honorable, isn't it?

My teenage years were filled with work. Granddaddy, Esau, and I built fences, chopped wood, planted gardens, dug wells, repaired the old house, and tended livestock—all *after* we picked cotton or chopped beans or cleared timber off some white man's land. We never had a day off. Never. Even on Sundays, which Granddaddy called the Lord's day, we did something. Not like other days, but we always did something.

Every now and then, on a Friday or Saturday night, me and Esau would get with other boys and go to town and hang out in the back of Mr. Raymond's pool hall or stumble our way through the woods to Jake's Juke Joint. It was so far back in the woods you couldn't drive to it. You'd have to leave your car on the main road, if you had one, and walk about a mile deep into the forest. Most people didn't have cars, so they walked from home. But they came. Oh, boy did they come! We tiptoed through the dark in our work boots then traded them, once we arrived, for our good shoes, which we had carried in our hands. The place was an old hay barn, big enough for a raggedy upright piano, a little raised wooden stage, and a dance floor that held fifty people or so. The music would be so loud you could hear it from the main road, but no authorities ever came back there. It was the darkness they feared. No one used flashlights or lanterns to get there. That was our way of protecting the place. There was no beaten path or signposts. For those of us who knew the land, we knew the dark and it knew us, so it guided us right to Jake's on Friday and Saturday nights.

Sometimes there was live music, but most times we danced to a jukebox that spun the same ten songs all night. A woman named Miss Ethel Faye sold fried fish and pork chop sandwiches for a quarter. She shoulda been a millionaire, the way folks ate in there. I don't know what she seasoned her food with, but couldn't nobody fry fish like Miss Ethel Faye. She sold drinks, too. Soda pop of every flavor, and beer and wine to grown folks. We didn't have age requirements for drinking back then, so when we said grown, we meant anyone who could handle a day's work. That was usually folks over fifteen or so. I didn't care much for alcohol—neither did Esau—but I liked smoking, so that's what I did.

Some nights we danced so hard the walls trembled. Nobody was shy about it. Even Esau, who couldn't dance at all, found himself on the floor with us. He didn't say much, but he wiggled around a little as he smiled. There was no judgment. If you were bold enough to get there, you were bold enough to boogie. John Lee Hooker had a song called "Boogie Chillen," and every time they played it, folks went to twistin and twirlin like there was no tomorrow. I liked Sam Cooke and Ella Fitzgerald and some of the other blues singers, too, but that song never got old. Some nights it'd be one o'clock in the morning before they shut down. That was late back then, 'cause don't care how long you stayed out, you still had to work or go to church the next morning.

Yet, at Jake's, folks spent the night drinkin and cussin and courtin and carryin on. Bobby Joe and I always flirted with whatever girls we could find. Esau sat quietly in a corner, drinking Nehi peach soda and nibbling on Miss Ethel Faye's fish sandwiches. Sometimes girls would talk to him, and he'd flash that smile and they'd melt, but that was as far as it went. Bobby Joe was another story. He was bolder than any of us, so, at some point he'd disappear outside—usually with a girl we called Sweetie Pie—then we'd have to walk him home 'cause he'd be too drunk to get there alone. Yet he'd tear up that dance floor. Nobody could outdance Bobby Joe Watkins. His legs seemed to have no bones or cartilage at all. They flowed like water beneath him as his arms flailed like windmills. Some nights, when he got to goin, people would back away and let him have the floor all to himself. We'd hoot and holler as he floated back and forth, grinning and winking at every girl in the place. Sweetie Pie swore she was gon marry Bobby Joe, but Bobby Joe left Arkansas at eighteen and never thought about Sweetie Pie again.

I loved goin to the shack because I loved music. I couldn't sing a lick or play any instrument, but I could sway pretty good and laugh my cares away. I enjoyed watching people unwind, shouting or singing lyrics they'd heard a thousand times. These were the same people who, during the day, were mean and rigid.

Then, one day, in the summer of 1956, Esau got sick. We were cutting wood with a crosscut saw, and suddenly he collapsed. "Esau!" I screamed and ran to his side. He was dazed and covered with sweat. He squeezed my arm and mumbled, "I'm okay, li'l brother. Just get me home." So I put his arm around my shoulders and walked him back to the house. I cried the whole way. I couldn't understand what was wrong with him.

Grandma told me to lay him on the bed and draw some cool water from the well. She was concerned, but not overly worried. He'd had fevers before. In fact, when he was little, he had Walkin Pneumonia, and folks thought he was gon die, but he didn't. It left him with a little cough that got bad sometimes in the winter but pretty much disappeared during the summer. That day, he was coughing pretty bad and breathing heavily. But he was also conscious and talking, so we thought he'd be all right. I sighed and walked outside and prayed like I'd never prayed before.

When Granddaddy came in from the field, he looked at Esau and shook his head. He told me to get the doctor right away.

"What's the matter with him, Granddaddy?" I murmured, trying not to cry.

"Do what I say!" he shouted, frantically.

I sprinted two and half miles to Doc Jenkins's place. When we got back, he told everyone to get out of the room and let him work.

We sat perfectly silent and still. I'm not sure I breathed at all. When Doc came out of the room, an eternity later, he said, "Could go either way. Keep a cool towel on his forehead. Gotta break that fever. Let him rest a little while. See if you can get something down his throat. A little soup or something."

I began to whimper. Granddaddy shot me a glance that made me restrain myself. All evening I drew fresh water from the well, over and over, so he'd have the coolest water possible. Grandma fanned Esau and whispered prayers directly into his eyes while Granddaddy went around the community, trying to collect outstanding debts so he could buy medicine or take Esau to the hospital. For a while, it seemed we had the fever under control, but by morning, Esau's pillow was wet with sweat. I screamed when I felt it and saw moisture all over his face. Grandma and Granddaddy came running. They told me to go get Doc Jenkins again, and, like the first time, I think I ran nonstop. After he examined Esau this time, he came out of the room, shaking his head.

"I don't know. I just don't know." He knew, but he didn't want to say.

"I can't lose my boy," Granddaddy said, more as a demand than a statement.

"Nothin else I can do, Abraham."

Granddaddy spoke louder: "Ain't no otha medicine, no surgery or nothin?"

Doc shook his head. Grandma covered her mouth and shivered. I started praying again. My brother was not going to die. I wouldn't have it. I told God I'd do anything—even preach, which I'd vowed *never* to do—if He would save my brother. I believed God heard my cry.

Esau made it through the day and, again, his fever seemed to wane. Grandma made sassafras tea and kept the cold compress against his forehead. Fevers were common back then, and folks knew how to fight them. Grandma scrambled around the clock, doing first one thing then another to restore Esau's health. We knew something serious was wrong when, three days later, he woke again, coughing softly and soaked with sweat.

He tried to deny things. Even joined us at the breakfast table. Grandma fussed the whole time. Granddaddy told her to leave him be. *Let him do what he can, woman.* Sweat poured as he ate slowly, painfully, but no one stopped him. I couldn't look at him. I knew this was something that couldn't be fixed, but I didn't want to admit it. Esau wanted to go to the field, but Granddaddy wouldn't let him. "Just take it easy, boy, and get well. That's yo job today."

Before noon, Grandma summoned us back into the house. Esau was vomiting blood and coughing violently. They sent me after the doctor again.

He stayed in the room with Esau a long time. The rest of us waited in the small living room, hoping for a miracle that wouldn't come.

When the doctor exited, he said, "I don't know, y'all. Could go either way. Just keep the cool rag on his forehead and try to get some soup in him." He shook his head and left.

At first, we didn't move. Then Granddaddy grabbed his hat from the nail on the wall and returned to the field. I stayed inside, trying to get Esau to swallow some broth, but he wouldn't take it.

At one point, he clutched my arm firmly and whispered, "I'll always be with you, little brotha. Always."

I dropped the soup to the floor and screamed, "NOOOOO!" as Esau took his final breath. Grandma shouted for Granddaddy to come. He already knew.

I ran past him, out the front door, as he mumbled, "De Lawd giveth and de Lawd taketh away. Blessed be the name of de Lawd." I didn't bless the name of the Lord that day. Instead, I yelled, "You promised me You'd heal him! I told You I'd do anything You want. I thought prayer changes things?"

It didn't that day. I've never forgiven God. I never will.

The days after Esau's death were dark and quiet. I couldn't eat. I couldn't sleep. I couldn't breathe normally. I didn't wash myself. I couldn't focus on anything. I stopped speaking. I never knew death could consume you like that.

Grandma begged me to say something, but had I opened my mouth, I would've wailed uncontrollably, so I kept my grief inside. Granddaddy didn't say anything. I saw him one evening, leaning against the side of the smokehouse, staring into nothing. He'd never been that pensive, so I waited a long while, wondering what he was thinking. Then I made a noise that brought him back to reality. Only then did he turn and brush something from his eye.

That's how it happened in the country sometimes. A person just got sick and died. No real explanation. We knew the limits of medicine and science, and most accepted them without question.

People said everyone's got a time to die. Prayers, medicine, or whatever can't change that. But I didn't believe it was Esau's time. I don't believe that now. I don't think Grandma believed it either. She cursed through her grief: "This don't make no damn sense! Why the hell God gotta take everythang you love?" It was the only time I'd heard her swear. Her concoctions, which we'd always trusted, had failed.

The day Esau died, a part of me died with him. If church folks are right, I'll see him soon and I'll be happy again. If they're wrong, I'll have no peace in eternity. No peace at all.

It rained the day we buried my brother. That's how I remember it. Grandma had said it was cloudy but never rained. Memory is such a funny thing.

We rode the old wagon to the church—Grandma with an umbrella, Granddaddy and me with our wide-brimmed hats—and walked through the double doors behind that shiny gray casket. I do not remember who was there. Or what folks said. Or what the choir sang. Or who preached the eulogy. I do not recall viewing Esau's body. Or what they served at the repast. Or whether folks hollered out loud or wept quietly. All I remember is that shiny gray casket lowering into the earth as the rain beat it angrily.

Granddaddy turned to me, once the grave was filled in, and said, "You on your own now," then walked back to the church.

I stood still, arms folded, rocking back and forth, as the storm cried for me.

NOVEMBER 21ST, 2003

Eventually, I spoke again but mostly to Grandma. She became my confidant. We'd sit at the small round kitchen table at night, talking about this, that, or the other or cooking something for the next day. Grandma's food was the best I've ever tasted. Hands down. People came from all over the community for her pound cake, sweet potato pie, fried cabbage, pork roast, blackberry cobbler, and practically anything else she cooked. Granddaddy warned others playfully to keep they ass away from his house, but they came anyway, especially on holidays. Grandma always cooked more than we could eat, so others tasted and sampled without hearing his mouth. After Esau died, she taught me many of her secrets. "No need takin 'em to de grave," she said.

One Saturday night, she motioned for me to follow her to the kitchen. Granddaddy rocked in his rocker, listening to the *Amos and Andy* radio show.

"Git de mixin bowl from up yonda," she said, tying an apron around her waist. I didn't get an apron. I was a boy. "Then get the flour, sugar, bakin power, and eggs and sit 'em on the table."

I obeyed, tasting the moist, lemony cake long before we cooked it.

She started humming something about flying away, then sat before the ingredients and winked.

"All right now. Measure out four cups o' flour." She handed me the measuring cup. She added several teaspoons of baking powder to it. Next, she reached into the bottom cabinet and got the sifter.

"First thang is this: always sift yo flour. Clumps make yo cake heavy and dry."

I didn't see the wisdom until I did it. Little stones of dried flour remained in the screened sifter after the good flour fell through. She tossed the stones into the trash.

"Okay. Now take these two sticks o' butter and mix 'em in wit yo flour."

"Why they so soft?"

"'Cause you gotta melt yo butter first or yo cake be lumpy."

Only then did I realize she'd taken the butter out sometime earlier that day.

"Gotta think ahead o' yoself, son."

We laughed together. I mashed the butter into the flour thoroughly until it gelled like clay.

"Okay. That's good, that's good. Now add a cup o' milk."

I got the bottle from the icebox and measured out a cup.

"It ain't got to be exact," she teased. "Just fill the measurin cup and let it spill over a li'l into the bowl."

"That's the secret, huh?"

She nudged me playfully. "Anything good is trial and error, boy. Don't neva fugit that." She winked again.

"Now mix it around wit yo hands."

"My hands?" I screeched.

"Dat's right. There's flava in yo hands. You didn't know dat, did you?"

I shook my head and frowned.

"Well, go 'head on."

I sighed and buried my hands into the mixture, moving everything around until the milk, flour, and butter flowed together.

"I'm gon add three and a half cups o' sugar now." She did that and instructed me to keep on mixin. I liked the feeling, the cool moisture oozing between my rough, skinny fingers.

"Okay. Now take yo hands out and let 'em drip real good. You wanna keep all the batter you can."

She slung an old kitchen rag over my shoulder and told me to wash my hands. After that, she called me back to the table.

"Now this is the important part." She lifted the carton of eggs. "We gon use nine eggs."

"Nine eggs?"

"That's right. Why you think folks be sniffin round here when I get done?"

I cackled. "You right about that!"

"I know I'm right!" she sang. "But the catch is you gotta add one egg at a time. Then beat it into the mixture, then add the next one, and so on and so forth."

"Why?"

"Make yo batter creamy and even. It'll rise right if you do dat. If you don't, yo cake be lopsided."

"Gee, Grandma, how you learn all dis?"

"By bakin plenty lopsided cakes!"

We hollered so loud Granddaddy grumbled, "What cha'll doin in dere, carryin on so?"

This was one time we ignored him.

I whipped the batter quickly with the large stirring spoon as Grandma cracked each shell so clean you could've put the egg back in it. She did this with one swift hit on the edge of the bowl. I tried it, but the entire shell crumbled.

"You hit it too hard. Gotta be gentle *and* firm. Most folks is one or the other."

I didn't have the touch, so I let her do the cracking as I continued stirring. The mixture became thicker and thicker until, soon, it was a smooth, buttery sea. I switched hands when my right hand tired out.

"Cookin's a lotta work, boy. You better believe that."

Now I knew why she, too, was exhausted at night.

"Most folks just put vanilla extract in they pound cake, but I put a teaspoon of vanilla and a teaspoon of lemon. Give it a better flavor."

I tried hard to remember everything she was telling me. "You got this wrote down somewhere, Grandma?"

"Yeah," she said. "In my heart. That's where you better put it, too. Can't nobody take yo heart from you." She nodded slowly, giving me time to comprehend her words. I didn't.

"Okay. Let's see what you done done," she said and ran her finger along the top edge of the mixture then stuck it in her mouth and closed her eyes.

I stared and waited.

She turned suddenly and got a lemon from the icebox. "Roll dat round on de table wit yo hand. Don't press too hard or you'll bust it open and lose yo juice. Jes git it soft."

I'd never rolled a lemon in my life, but as I did, I felt its skin loosen beneath my touch. After a minute or so, I handed it back to Grandma, who cut the top open and squeezed a quick stream into the batter. "That oughta do it!" she said.

I stirred a bit longer and she tasted again. "Yep. That was it. You got yoself somethin now!"

She laid a soft, approving hand on my shoulder.

"Okay. Now you gotta grease yo pan. Git it down from the top shelf up there."

I obeyed.

"Take you a li'l oil and make sure you grease it good. Don't leave no dry spots."

I did that while she added a little whippin cream to the batter. "This make yo cake mo moist. Jes a li'l bit. Don't take much."

I showed her the greased pan. She nodded.

"Put you some flour in there and knock it around until the whole pan is white."

I spilt flour on the table and floor, but Grandma didn't reprimand me. She said, "Never mind that. You'll clean it up later. That's part of the process."

My arm was so tired I could hardly lift it. Grandma laughed at me as I bent it back and forth.

"Take yo bowl and pour yo batter all around the pan. Then scrape what's left, too." She paused. "When you git yo chillen, leave enough for them to lick."

Esau and I used to fidget whenever Grandma baked, waiting for the mixin bowl. "All right, boys," she'd call. "Come on!" and we'd scamper into the kitchen and sit at the table, running our fingers over the bottom and sides of the wooden container till it squeaked. I never knew she intentionally left our portion.

"I heated the oven befo' we started," she sassed, proving, once again, that she'd out-thought me.

We cackled and chuckled while the cake rose in the old woodstove. Grandma told me about her parents, who were from a little place called Coldwater, Mississippi. When slavery ended, they migrated to Arkansas, having heard that white folks were paying Negroes almost a dollar a day to pick cotton. It was a lie. But they'd spent their money to get there, so they stayed and made a living. She had four older sisters, three of whom died before she got grown. The one who lived died right after my mother. "She used to come up here all the time and stay with me," Grandma recalled. "You think I can cook? Now Helen Faye could cook!" She told me all about her and her one son who left and worked on the railroad. "After his momma died, he went to California and disappeared. Never did hear from him no mo. Don't know what happened to 'im."

I promised I'd look him up one day, but I never did.

We laughed and talked till Grandma said, "Git a straw from the broom and stick it in the cake. If it come out clean, it's done." It had a few particles on it, so we left the cake in the oven another ten minutes. "It's done now," she said, so I took it from the oven and set it on top of the stove.

"Let it cool a few minutes, then we'll take it outta the pan."

The lemony aroma filled the house. Granddaddy said, "Shit! Somethin smellin good in dere!" Grandma showed me how to lay a plate on top of the Bundt pan and turn it upside down. She eased the pan upward, and the cake sat tall upon the throne, all muddy-brown and pretty. My eyes gleamed. "You got yoself somethin there, boy!" she declared, shaking her head and smiling. I've rarely been so proud. When I cut a piece and lifted it, moisture leaked into my hands. Years later, your mother and I tried, over and over again, to make that cake, but it never came out right. We were always missing something.

Grandma died a year after Esau—the day before my seventeenth birthday. Cancer, the doctor guessed. She'd told me a week earlier that, if she could do it over again, she might not marry Granddaddy. He heard her but didn't care. He buried her without remorse. The funeral occurred on a sunny Saturday morning at nine because, as he told a few nosey neighbors, "Got things to do. Can't spend a whole day on what I can't change. Best do what I can while I can."

Granddaddy sat perfectly upright during the funeral. Folks shook his hand as they passed by, nodding sympathies and condolences. Granddaddy reminded them that "We all gotta go this way. Better get ready." He never dropped a tear. Neither did I. I felt it though, that grief stirring at the bottom of my belly. Only when Miss Ira Lou belted Grandma's theme song, "'Some glad morning, when this life is o'er, I'll fly away,'" did I stir a bit, but I shook my head and cleared my throat until it subsided.

At the graveside, before lowering the casket into the

ground, funeral officiates asked, "Would anyone have any last words?" I pondered a moment, then began to rise, but Granddaddy beat me to it.

"It's appointed unto man once to die, then the judgment," he said sternly, glancing at the tops of bowed heads. "Better get your house in order. No man knows the day nor the hour the son of man cometh. He cometh like a thief in the night, seeking whom he may devour." Granddaddy paused, believing in his own profundity. Then he switched his tone: "Tomorrow ain't promised to nobody. If you got somethin to do, better go 'head and do it. Fool round too long, and you'll leave it undone." Heads nodded as people mumbled, "Amen, amen." There was nothing for me to say.

Everyone returned to the church but Granddaddy and me. He took a handful of earth and crumbled it over the casket, resting deep in the ground. I did the same. Minutes passed as we thought private thoughts but shared nothing. A little brown sparrow descended onto the mound of fresh dirt next to the grave, leaned its head back, and began chirping in quick, single notes. Granddaddy, with his smooth, easy bass, joined in:

When the shadows of this life have gone,
I'll fly away!
Like a bird from prison bars has flown,
I'll fly away!
I'll fly away! Oh, glory, I'll fly away
When I die, Hallelujah by and by,
I'll fly away!

Together, they sang a duet of mourning. I only listened, having no vocal capacity whatever, as the old man and the sparrow finished what Miss Ira Lou had begun. Then, as quickly as it had come, it lifted into the air, higher and higher, until disappearing behind a cluster of oak trees. Granddaddy turned to me as if he might say something personal, something he'd been holding all morning, but instead he laid a heavy hand upon my shoulder and said, "Time to go." We walked, side by side, down the grassy lane, back to the old house.

We changed into work clothes and met back at the front door. "You gon do the cookin from now on," he said. "If you stay here. If you don't, I'll manage." He walked to the field without my response.

It was 1957. I didn't leave. Not right away. There was nowhere to go. We simply reordered our silent world and continued living. I'd learned to cook from Grandma on rainy days. She made the fluffiest, sweetest biscuits I've ever tasted. Mine turned out okay, but not like hers. Granddaddy ate them anyway. The hardest part about cooking for a country man is getting up before him to do it. The day after we buried Grandma, I rose at six and rushed to the kitchen, only to find Granddaddy fully dressed at the table, rubbing his short, scruffy beard. "Mornin," I said. He glanced up and said, "Mornin been gone."

Within minutes, I placed three strips of bacon, two scrambled eggs, and a couple of pieces of toast before him. There was no time for biscuits. He inhaled the food quickly, rose and grabbed his hat from a nail on the wall, and went to the field. I began thinking about supper. Breakfast was never late again.

Yet don't be deceived: I was not cooking while Grand-daddy worked in the field. I prepared meals, yes, but when dishes were washed and the next meal underway, I was expected in the field, too. I was a man, after all, required to do a man's day.

Granddaddy and I didn't talk much during those latter years. We did our work, ate, and went to bed without so much as a sentence some days. Yet I heard that he'd been quite the talker, quite the ladies' man, once upon a time. Some said he'd cheated on Grandma. I didn't want to believe that, but there was no way to know, since no fool in his right mind would've asked him about it.

I was almost that fool once. We were fishing on the old riverbank in early spring, when fish come shallow to spawn. I'd heard enough about Granddaddy's escapades, so I decided to ask the old man myself. I was eighteen or so, and rather tall—almost Granddaddy's height—with fresh whiskers sprouting from my chin, so I was ready. Or so I thought.

I tossed my line next to a gathering of lily pads and started murmuring, "Um…Granddaddy…I…um…wanna…" but I couldn't get it out. Granddaddy didn't look at me. I suppose he waited for me to be man enough to say what I wanted to say. But I couldn't.

Instead he said, "Speak yo mind, boy. Or let it 'lone."

I didn't intend to be intimidated, so I regathered my nerves and started again: "Is it true…um…what people say…"

He cut me off: "Folks talk shit all the time bout stuff they don't know, boy. Be careful listenin to other folks. If you ain't seen it for yourself, it probably ain't so."

But it was so! I believed it. Everybody believed it.

Minutes passed in a gruesome, tortuous silence. My nerve was slipping away.

Suddenly, I snagged a huge crappie, but my line broke and it got away. Granddaddy said, "Why did your line snap?"

"Because he was too heavy."

"No sir. It snapped because you made a mistake—you didn't put new line on the poles like I told you to."

I'd forgotten that.

"Now it cost you everything."

I sighed.

"A man is gon pay for his mistakes, boy. One way or the other. Good Lawd gon make sure of that."

Granddaddy turned, finally, and stared at me. I understood. I repaired my line and tossed it back into the water. I had no further questions.

I stayed with Granddaddy until I was twenty-one, which is a long time in the country. I think I feared leaving him alone. Or maybe I was too scared to venture out on my own. I don't know. But one evening, rocking in his rocker, listening to the old radio, he said out of the blue, "Ain't you found no woman yet?" I shrugged and said, "Ain't no girls round here." He cackled and said, "Sometime, you gotta go where they is." I nodded, understanding him to be saying it was time for me to go.

That was the summer of '61, I believe, the year I met your mother. She visited your great-aunt Loretha in our hometown, and I couldn't take my eyes off her. I'd heard from local boys how pretty she was, with long shapely legs, but I'd never seen her. She'd come down to Arkansas plenty of times, but usually during her visits I was keeping the homestead. By the time I got word of her presence, she'd be gone. Word traveled slowly back in those days, especially as far out as we lived, so I didn't think much about her. But the day I saw her at church, in a pleated white dress and wide-brimmed lavender hat, I almost bit my bottom lip off. She was something to behold. Tallish, five-eight or so, and curvy as a winding stream. Her hair lay straight back in a ponytail with a white ribbon holding it together. Every feature on her face was proportionate: penny-size eyes with long lashes, plump lips covered with red lipstick, and a light brownish complexion as smooth and even as peanut butter. I lifted my hand to touch her face, then clutched it to my side. She smiled and made me smile, and I didn't know what to do. I knew I wanted her. There was nothing in the world I wanted more. Granddaddy saw my affection and said, "Bout time, boy! Shit!" Later at home he added, "A woman's a mighty thang. What you see ain't always what you get." I understood what he meant, but I was already in love. I had to have her. I *would* have her. Somehow, some way, I would have her.

I was six-one, stout and muscular from farm labor, so I guess I wasn't a bad catch either. It was the church anniversary that Sunday, which meant we shared dinner together in the dining hall. I weaseled next to your mother, who acted as if she didn't see me, but she did.

"Hello," I said softly.

She smiled without looking at me. "Hello."

"You're Miss Loretha's niece?"

"Yes I am."

"I'm Jacob Swinton."

"I know who you are. I've heard about you."

I smiled. "What have you heard?"

"Just *things*."

She didn't intend to elaborate, so I didn't press the matter. "What's your name?"

"Rachel."

"That's a pretty name."

I wanted to engage her more, but my mind went blank. After several minutes of crunchy fried chicken and potato salad, I asked, "Can I come see you sometime?"

She smirked playfully. "Sure. If you want to."

"I do!"

When she chuckled, I saw the prettiest, deepest-set dimples I'd ever seen. I grabbed my thighs to keep my hands still. I couldn't touch her. Not yet. We didn't do that back in my day. At least not on the first date. And usually not until marriage. No one thinks that way anymore.

I went to Miss Loretha's almost every evening at sundown. She lived right off the highway, behind Smirl's Grocery store. Do you remember that store? I can't recall if it was still there when I used to take you down home. Anyway, Miss Loretha's house, like a mighty throne, sat high and proud upon cinderblocks. She didn't have kids—none that I knew of—and her sister, Cora, your grandmother, lived in Kansas City. She'd send your mother down to stay with your great-aunt awhile each year, sometimes a week or two, sometimes the whole summer, and that year, it was the whole summer.

When I arrived the first evening, sporting my good overalls, your mother was sitting on the edge of the porch. Miss Loretha lounged in a rocking chair with a dishrag slung over her shoulder for flies and mosquitoes. She was a pretty woman, too. They shared a reddish tint, which everyone assumed to be Indian blood. It might've been. All I knew was that I liked it.

The house was perfectly white with a row of golden marigolds just below the front porch. As I approached, Miss Loretha waved and hollered, "Bout time you got over here to see me!" Of course I wasn't there to see her, and she knew it, so she made some excuse about checking on a pot of greens, and disappeared into the house. Your mother blushed and looked away, but I'd walked too far to be timid.

"How you doin?" I said.

"Doin fine," she whispered.

A sweet, intoxicating fragrance hovered around her.

"What's your whole name?"

She cleared her throat. "Rachel Marie White. Some people call me Marie."

"I like Rachel. I think it's prettier."

"Suit yourself," she sassed, flirtatiously. "It's up to you."

"Well, nice to see you again, Miss Rachel."

"Nice to see you, too, Mr. Jacob Swinton."

"How old are you?" I asked.

"Seventeen. How old are you?"

"Twenty," I said proudly.

We nodded, unaware of how to proceed. I can't remember what we said next, but soon Miss Loretha called us in for a plate of greens, salted meat, and cornbread. Nobody's greens beat Miss Loretha's. And I mean *nobody's*. People asked what she put in them, but she never would say. I asked that day, too, thinking I might get lucky, but she told me playfully to mind my own business. So the three of us chatted awhile longer, sitting in the living room. That's how young folks courted back then.

By the time I left, it was pitch-dark. I'd convinced myself she liked me—a feeling I'd never known before. From my folks' example, marriage was having babies and raising them together. I didn't know anything about love. I certainly hadn't seen it—mutual affection between adults—and I wasn't sure how it worked, but I liked the way it made me feel—warm inside, worthy of life. The way a man is supposed to feel with a woman. And I never wanted that feeling to end.

It was late—after ten—when I got home, but the four-mile walk was worth it. Every minute in your mother's presence was a blessing. That probably sounds cheesy to you, but it meant everything to me. When she laughed, I smiled and tingled inside. This was all new, but I loved it. I felt *desired*, son. Attractive. For a poor Negro country boy like me, that was a new experience. The walk was an hour each way, but I never thought about the time. I realize now that I loved her because she liked me—not because of who she was. I didn't really know your mother until we'd been married many years. Courting the way we did didn't reveal deep levels of knowing. So perhaps our way of romance wasn't as excellent as I'd thought. Nonetheless, we were young and in love, and I was happy.

"Sometimes I wanna kiss you," I said one evening, staring at the stars. It was dusky, but not dark. Miss Loretha had just excused herself into the house. Mosquitoes buzzed around our ears, but they didn't deter me.

Her silence suggested she hadn't heard me, but after a moment she said, "Who's stopping you?"

I didn't move. My rock-solid confidence began to melt away. Sweat broke across my brow, and my heart started beating fast. I knew if I didn't do it soon, I never would, but I was scared. Women were delicate, precious things, I'd been taught, and I didn't want to mess up. Boys had teased me about being a virgin, which I was, but I had kissed girls before. Still, they weren't your mother. She was different. Classy. Elegant. Smart. Citified. I was a country boy who could barely read, and she wanted *me*?

I huffed one good time, looked around to make sure Miss Loretha wasn't watching, and stepped toward your mother. She giggled, but stared into my eyes. Then, slowly, my head lowered, hers raised, and our lips met. It was sweet, the taste of her mouth, soft and moist like Grandma's lemon pound cake.

When we released and I opened my eyes, I saw that she was crying.

"What's wrong?" I asked.

"Nothin. I'm fine," she whispered, wiping tears. "Just… happy."

That meant I could kiss her again, so I did. This time, I caressed her back as her hands massaged my waist, and in that moment I couldn't have imagined anything more wonderful.

We started *going together*—that was the term we used back then. I was her boyfriend; she was my girl. Granddaddy said, "Aw shit, Miss Agnes!" when he heard the news, meaning he was happy for me. I laughed at his affirmation because, finally, we were men together, and I'd waited a long time for that.

Each day I took your mother a different flower. Most grew

wild in the woods behind our house, so they weren't hard to find. She began to be amazed at the sheer variety, as if, overnight, I was creating them myself. I liked that I possessed knowledge of something she didn't—the land. Her citified ways, language, references had intimidated me at first, but once I discovered her ignorance of the country, I got my confidence back and taught her all sorts of things like the difference between purple hull and whip-poor-will peas; how to distinguish field corn from sweet corn; how to recognize collard, mustard, and kale greens; the difference between a mule and a donkey. She taught me things, too: that *unthaw* is not a word; that Egypt is an African country; that Abraham Lincoln did *not* willingly free the slaves; that a black woman had become a millionaire from straightening hair. I was as fascinated with her knowledge as she was with mine. We were perfectly complementary, it seemed—until we got married.

These were the kinds of things I wanted to share with you. Man things. Things a father ought to tell his son. But you weren't interested. Even as a little boy, you thought I was cold and mean. Perhaps I was. But I was a *man*. I was a man the way I'd been taught to be a man. People respected that. I stayed on the same job forty years because of it. I supported you and your mother because of it. I own a house because of it. You have an inheritance because of it. Never did I think I'd have to apologize for being a man. But, like I said, the world changed faster than I could.

NOVEMBER 23RD, 2003

I left Blackwell for Kansas City the following spring. Granddaddy was in good health, so I believed he could survive
without me. My heart was in your mother's hands; hers in
mine. I promised Granddaddy to visit soon. And often. He
nodded and told me to do what I had to do. We didn't hug
or shake hands or anything. We simply turned and walked
in opposite directions.

I rode to Kansas City with Bobby Joe. He'd been there
a few years, working at the Folger Coffee Company, and
every few months he'd come home and check on his folks.
He had a rusty '57 Chevy, which I loved and drove around
until I got my job at the post office and bought my own car.
I'd never been to a city before. When we arrived, I knew
I'd never leave. Buildings everywhere, businesses on every
corner, people walking about casually, cars and trucks blar-
ing horns, houses lined like matchboxes. And no dirt roads?

Arkansas was for the birds! I'd see Granddaddy at Christmas, I told myself.

What I liked most about Kansas City was that there was always something to do. On Friday or Saturday nights, we'd go to black clubs downtown where blues and jazz artists played. That's how I saw B.B. King live. I loved the blues because most songs were about hard living, and I knew something about that. I saw other singers, too, like Bobby "Blue" Bland. He wasn't very popular then, but he had a smooth, clean voice I liked, especially when he sang "Cry, Cry, Cry." That was my song. I'd hum it at the post office to get me through the day or whenever your mother made me mad. Sometimes I'd go to the club by myself, find a dark corner and smoke the night away. Other times, after I met a few fellas, we'd go together and laugh and clown. Almost every blues singer in the 1960s and '70s came through Kansas City, and I bet I heard most of them live.

I was a sports fan, too, as you know, so I loved going to Kansas City Royals and Chiefs games. Things weren't quite as segregated in Kansas City as they were in Arkansas—although the racism was just as bad—so black people could enjoy outings just like white people.

My favorite hobby was fishing. You and your mother didn't like it, so usually I went alone. I took you once though. Do you remember that? You were probably seven or eight or so. You cried all the way to Perry Lake. I spanked you when we arrived and told you to get it together. You hushed, but your misery was obvious. I fished all day long just to torture you. We never went again.

But I'm ahead of myself. Let me back up.

Bobby Joe married a girl from Raytown, Missouri, named Marilyn. Do you remember her? I know you remember Bobby Joe, but you might not remember Marilyn. She was sweet as could be. Died of a brain aneurism when you were four or five. Used to watch you sometimes when your mother and I went out. You could do no wrong in her eyes. Oh, how you loved that woman! I stayed with them about a month till I got my own place on Brooklyn Avenue. Just a room and a bathroom in the back of a house, but it was mine, so I was content.

Your mother lived close by, just off the corner of 57th and College. She was about to graduate from high school and was on her way to Oberlin in the fall. I worked nights, so when I got off in the mornings, I'd go straight to her house. Your grandma Cora liked me, so she always had breakfast ready when I arrived. Sometimes your mother cooked, too, but not often. She was a reader, a writer, who loved books and wrote poems in her spare time. I didn't always understand them, but I liked a few, especially the one about me. She swore it wasn't about me, but I know it was. It went like this:

Midnight stars dance in his eyes
And twinkle brighter when he comes—

In his arms, I am lifted higher, higher
Until beholding the world at a glance.

Saviors come and go,
But none has rescued the heart of a woman
Like he has—

He is hope, he is desire, he is every dream fulfilled—
And he is mine.

She said the poem was about Jesus, but I knew better. She read it to me every time I saw her. That's how I memorized it. When we divorced, I wrote it down since I'd never hear her say it again.

We dated that summer and she got pregnant. That's how we said it back then. Some men in your generation say *we're* pregnant, but we wouldn't have said that. Pregnancy was a woman's issue in my day, and if she were unmarried, it was a stain on her reputation. Such was the case with your mother. I know what I said earlier, that I wouldn't have touched her before marriage, and that was so—if we had stayed in the country. But in Kansas City, things were different. People didn't mind other folks' business the way they did back home. City folks might've frowned at what they knew, but they never would've condemned you for it.

Still, once she got pregnant, I knew I had to marry her. That was nonnegotiable. I'd wanted to marry her anyway; just not so soon. My plan had been to buy a house and a car before proposing, but that didn't happen. I never even proposed. She simply asked when I wanted to have the wedding. Granddaddy would've been disappointed. He'd told Esau and me that marriage comes *before* children. When children come first, he said, the marriage suffers. "Bible tells you to take a wife first and covet her." I wasn't sure the Bible said this, but since I wasn't a reader, I didn't care to find out. When your mother told me she was pregnant, I saw Granddaddy, in my mind, shaking his head. I've never been able to shake that image.

We married on June 13, 1962, in your grandma Cora's front yard. Your mother was the most beautiful bride I'd ever seen. Sleek white dress with just enough train to anoint the ground. I was happy that day. Really happy. She wasn't showing yet, so from the looks of things, life was perfect. All her family was there, and, as you know, she has a large one. Uncle Money, Uncle Theo, Uncle Charles, Aunt Merle, Aunt Clarissa, and all their children, drinking and talking shit as your mother came down the aisle. Those are some crazy folks, son. At least they were then. They drank alcohol like water. When your mother and I visited them, there was always a bar loaded with liquor. I was never much of a drinker, as you know, but your mother's folks were. They guzzled all day long. They'd appear tipsy sometimes, but never drunk. I didn't understand it. And they drank hard stuff: bourbon, Scotch, brandy, vodka. Took it straight, too. That's one of the reasons your mother and I didn't make it. But at the time we were happy.

We moved into this house two weeks later. I'd driven by it months earlier and liked it because it was green. That's my favorite color. Sorta reminds me of young crops in spring. The door and shutters were white. I liked most the huge lawn where I dreamed our children would play. I didn't worry whether your mother would like it or not. She would like it. Any woman would. I was doing what Granddaddy had taught me, and I felt proud of that. The huge rosebush just to the left of the front door was barely a twig back then, and the willow tree, which you liked so much, was just a young sapling. It wasn't a mansion by any means; it was a quaint little house, sort of like a country cottage, where I thought I could raise a family. And I did.

All the houses on the street were the same style but different colors. It was a new neighborhood, and I liked that. I didn't want somebody else's old house, filled with their good or bad memories. I wanted a new place, something untouched by others' hands, a home no one had owned but me. I guess growing up in the country spoiled me in that way. I saw the for sale sign and called the Realtor. We went back and forth a bit because I didn't have quite enough money saved, but Bobby Joe helped me out. When your mother saw it, she covered her mouth and cried. "Our own home," she whispered. I smiled because she was happy, and that's what I'd wanted— to make her happy.

She got out of the car and stood on the sidewalk, staring as if looking at Heaven. She looked at the house, the perfectly cut lawn, the brand-new fence, and suddenly jumped into my arms. "Oh, Jacob! It's beautiful! It's just beautiful!" I couldn't stop smiling. The Realtor pulled up shortly and gave her a tour of the inside. Again, it wasn't grand, but it was hers and she was thrilled. She loved the kitchen, she said, with the little bay window. I liked that, too. Light streamed through in beams of glory, and we knew this was where we were supposed to be. The rest of the house was fine: three small bedrooms, two baths, and a decent-size living room. What more could we want?

NOVEMBER 27TH, 2003

It's Thanksgiving Day—cold, cloudy, and lonely. I had enough strength to scramble an egg and make some toast this morning, so that's what I ate. No turkey and dressing for me. My family's gone and I don't want anyone else's pity.

If you still don't understand why I'm telling you all this, just keep reading. A man's history is all he has. It says more than his mouth ever will. You'll see what I mean soon enough.

I got the call, three weeks after the wedding, that Granddaddy had died. Someone found him facedown in the pea patch. I'd wondered how I'd react on that day, if I'd cry or shiver with grief, but I did neither. I laughed instead. This might sound strange, but it's what I felt. He died doing precisely what he liked. He died on the land. It was like him to have his way, to make Death come for him in the middle of the field. That's why I laughed, because Granddaddy had the last word—as usual.

When I arrived home the next day, folks stood around everywhere, cackling and gossiping, as was our custom. Your mother and I exited the car, and suddenly people formed a circle around us and hugged us tightly. Men jerked my hand so hard I thought it might separate from my arm. They meant well. It was their way of loving me, of extending condolences to Abraham Swinton's last living immediate relative. Mr. Erby, one of Granddaddy's oldest friends, said, "Let's bow in a word of prayer," and prayed five minutes, which is a long, long time to pray. When he finished, the circle disintegrated, and people returned to their boisterous chatter.

I looked at the house. It seemed frozen in time. No one had entered since finding Granddaddy in the field. They laid his body on a cooling board on the back porch. I teared but didn't cry. Instead, I closed my eyes and leaned against the nearest wall as memories crystallized in my mind. I recalled that, every Thanksgiving, he stood before we ate and said grace more thoroughly than on other days. I'd stare at him and marvel that everything on the table—and I mean *everything*—came from the sweat of our hands. Tasted like it, too. To this day, I despise restaurant and packaged foods because they never taste as good as what we grew.

This was all because of Granddaddy. Grandma had dreamed, she'd said, of eating at a restaurant in town, one of the few that served Colored people. I think she simply wanted to know the feeling of being served, but Granddaddy wouldn't go. He said we could go without him, but we never did, so the only food I ate came straight from the land. When

I moved to Kansas City and ate, for the first time, at a restaurant, I was sorely disappointed. Food tasted bland and old, and it cost far too much. Even grocery store meats and vegetables were a sad substitute for what I'd known. I understood, finally, Granddaddy's point.

Moving room to room, I'd forgotten how little we owned. A small ragged sofa, a rocking chair, the old high-back radio, a worn but sturdy cast-iron bed. The kitchen had a few warped pots hanging from nails on the wall. In the center of the table was Grandma's old ceramic mixing bowl, doused with flour. Granddaddy had probably started a few homemade biscuits the morning he died, then decided against it. I wiped the bowl clean and washed it out. I'd take that with me. Everything else could stay right where it was. I'd be back, I told myself.

Then came the hard part—viewing Granddaddy's body. Poor black folks like us couldn't afford embalming and funeral homes, so our undertaker—every community had one—came and cleaned the body and sprayed it with a slow-decaying substance, then returned it to the cooling board until we buried it. Granddaddy had on his ragged overalls and work boots. I would change him into his good suit and Sunday shoes, which I'd first have to polish. As I stepped closer, I trembled a bit, then studied his face. He looked like himself. I had feared he'd look ashen and gray, like some dead people, but he didn't. I nodded approval and shook his hand as if greeting him formally, and that's when sorrow overwhelmed me—when I clutched his limp right hand. Granddaddy hated nothing more than a man's weak handshake, so I knew he was gone.

Tears came, but I restrained them. I wanted to collapse upon his body and thank him for taking Esau and me when no one else would. I wanted to assure him I knew how to work and that it had saved my life. I wanted to boast that I had a son coming, a boy of my own—I hoped you'd be a boy, I wanted you to be a boy—and that his name would be Isaac. Instead, I held my peace and bowed my head.

NOVEMBER 28TH, 2003

A month ago, confined to a hospital bed, I couldn't have said my name without collapsing from exhaustion. Then, with the help of umpteen drugs, I regained a little strength and they sent me home. "The outlook's not good," the doctor said. "Of course it isn't," I said. He told me to get lots of rest and eat whenever I could. "I'm dying, ain't I, doc?" He didn't lie or extend any sympathy. "Yes, Mr. Swinton, you are. Do you have any next of kin? Any children or relatives who might come and help you out?" I laughed. "Help me die?" He stared as if offended, then rolled me in a wheelchair to the exit. "I'm not coming back, doc. This is it. Thank you for everything." He shook my hand and walked away.

Most days, I lie on the old sofa in my pajamas, watching the news or maybe reruns of *The Andy Griffith Show*. Some days I'm so drugged I think I've already died. I haven't had a haircut in years. There isn't much left, just a little on each side and the back. My beard is scruffy and unkempt, too. It isn't very long. I was never one to grow much facial hair, although I always thought I'd like a beard.

Yesterday, or the day before, I passed the full-length mirror in the hallway and saw a skeletal version of myself. I stood there, wondering how this had happened to me, thinking of all the things I'd do differently if I could live again. It was useless thinking, of course. Nothing was about to change. Not for me. There are no do-overs in this life. Either you get it right or you wish you had.

Your mother and I stayed with your aunt Loretha and planned Granddaddy's obituary. I knew his story—enough of it—so I talked as she wrote. He would've hated a long service, so I scheduled a few songs and asked a few old men to speak what they knew about him.

The morning of the funeral, cars and trucks filled every possible parking space. I was happy about that. I'd never seen so many people in one place in Blackwell. Some had to stand outside because the church couldn't hold them. It was a bright July morning, warm but not hot. Not yet. People fanned out of habit and rocked long before the music began. And when it did, you would've thought the gates of Heaven had swung open. Everyone joined in singing:

There is a fountain, filled with blood
Drawn from Emmanuel's veins;
And sinners plunged, beneath the flood,
Lose all their guilty stains!

The service was loud and rowdy. Granddaddy's casket was black and plain, just as he would've preferred. He'd said a pine box would suit him just fine, but I would've been ashamed of that.

People rejoiced as if something wonderful had happened. They didn't fear Death; in fact, they treated her like an old, personal friend. There was no terror, no uncertainty of things. People sang songs and tapped feet in rhythm as the preacher spoke of Heaven as a man's just reward. I find it funny that, at funerals, all dead people go to Heaven, regardless of how they lived. Perhaps this is black people's way of rewarding themselves simply for having been black and survived—even for a while.

Mr. John Davies, Mr. Buckeye Williams, and Mr. Theodore Fletcher gave personal reflections of Granddaddy, revealing things I didn't know. Like the fact that he'd been the main architect of the church. A fire destroyed the original building, Mr. Davies said, and when menfolk gathered to rebuild it, they discovered that Abraham Swinton knew more about carpentry than anyone around. He didn't enjoy the work, so he didn't do it often, but he sho was good at it. And since the church was God's house, he felt obligated to do it. "Strongest building in this hyeah community!" he shouted, and people shouted "Amen!" back at him.

Mr. Buckeye claimed that, once upon a time, Granddaddy sang with a quartet called The Golden Jubilaires. I was surprised, but it made sense. Sometimes, on Saturday nights, in his heavy, rumbling bass, he'd listen to and sing along with the music on the old Zenith radio. Music made Granddaddy bearable. Happy. Even nice sometimes. His spirit settled when he sang, and me and Esau would sit quiet and still as mice until he finished.

What everyone said emphatically was that Granddaddy had been a hell of a man. They didn't mourn his passing as much as they mourned the passing of his manhood. "They don't make 'em like that anymore!" Mr. Fletcher said, and the crowd bellowed "Amen!" and "Sho you right!"

"That man could *worrrk*," he emphasized. "And Abraham was good at mindin his own business, too."

People praised Granddaddy throughout the service. I nodded along. But Granddaddy had also been rough and harsh and downright mean sometimes. Your mother rubbed my hand. She knew what I was thinking. She also knew this wasn't the time for it.

We buried Granddaddy next to Grandma, in Rose of Sharon Cemetery behind the church, and by sundown, your mother and I were headed back to Kansas City. She didn't feel well, so she slept most of the way. I spent hours wondering what kind of boy you'd be, who you'd look like, what you'd laugh about, what you might one day die for. I hoped you'd look like your uncle Esau.

But more, I hoped you'd love me just because I was your father.

NOVEMBER 29TH, 2003

We named you Isaac because it means "laughter," which Rachel and I hoped you'd always have. I liked the name because it came from the Bible. I didn't remember exactly who Isaac was, but I remembered Granddaddy talking about him. Folks down home often gave kids biblical names—Jeremiah, Moses, Daniel, Mary, Martha, Paul, Silas—because they believed the Bible to be the word of God. I believed that, too.

The day you were born was the happiest day of my life. I was twenty-two and had a son. I stood at the hospital nursery window for hours, staring at you, mumbling and waving as if you heard me.

In the coming weeks, I rushed home from work every day to hold you and tickle you until you smiled. Your mother smiled, too, watching us bond. She said we looked alike, but I thought you looked like Esau. I used to kiss you on the forehead every day.

You'd reach for me when I, sweaty and all, came through the door, and I'd grab you and swing you in the air until your mother warned me not to be so rough.

One evening, when you were a year old or so, you started crying and wouldn't stop. Rachel couldn't figure out what was wrong with you. She thought you were teething, which you were, but the pacifier did no good. With her index finger, she massaged your gums tenderly, but still you cried louder. She asked me if I thought we should take you to the emergency room, and I said no. Hospitals were never the answer to any childhood ailment I knew. Your mother was worried sick. She paced as you wept. Then something magical happened. I picked you up and laid you in the center of my chest and suddenly you stopped crying. I stretched out on the couch, flat on my back, with your little body right atop my heart. You breathed deeply for a while, exhausted from having screamed for hours, but you didn't cry anymore. I felt your little heartbeat. It was faster than mine. For every beat of my heart, yours beat twice. It was sorta like a drum duet—one hard, heavy thump accompanied by two light, crisp thumps that seemed musically composed. I closed my eyes and smiled as the rhythm played between us. Then I rubbed your back softly until we both drifted to sleep. For months, nothing calmed your crankiness except the complementary beating of our hearts.

I wished Granddaddy had seen you. I imagined myself handing you off to him as he rocked in his rocker, bouncing you upon his arthritic knees, listening to the old radio and humming along. Sometimes, a man softens with age and grandchildren. "You protect 'em and provide for 'em," he used to say. "Don't care what you gotta do. Just make sure you do it."

I spent your first year watching you grow and playing with you on the living room floor. Your mother would read novels or write poetry as we made ungodly noises throughout the house. How she concentrated I don't know, but she did.

When you were eight months or so, your mother started drinking. This turned our good times to bad times. I'd come home some evenings and find her unconscious across the sofa with you screaming in your crib. It scared me. We fought about it more than once, but she insisted she had things under control.

I came home late one night—you couldn't have been more than a year old or so—and found you soiled and starving. Rachel sat in the middle of the floor, slumped over. I kicked her thigh to arouse her, and when she awoke and tried to stand, I slapped her so hard she collapsed again. The longer I looked at her, the more disgusted I became. My fury boiled. She was supposed to be virtuous, upstanding, modest, and she wasn't. I felt as if she'd made a fool of me. The house wasn't nasty, but it wasn't clean either, and it should've been. She was home all day, and this meant the house should've been clean. That was a woman's role, I'd been taught. To cook and clean and iron and sew for her family. My role was to work. I did that, so she had no excuse.

As you know, she never made it to Oberlin. That's why she started drinking, I think. She'd abandoned her dream and became what the world said she should be. And she hated it. She didn't hate *you*. Or me. She loved you more than anything in the world. She just hated that she couldn't have both—

a family and a college degree. She never said this and she wouldn't have. She wasn't allowed. It was the mid-1960s, and all she'd ever really wanted was knowledge. She loved school like Granddaddy loved the land. I wasn't invested in education. I didn't see why anybody needed *that* much schooling.

It was my right, I thought, to remind your mother of her place. She'd agreed to this the day we married. She'd said, "I will" when the preacher asked if she would obey me. I took those vows seriously.

Sobering quickly, she screamed, "Stop it! Stop it!" but there was no stopping me.

"You will obey me!" I shouted, "and you will stop this drinking and start tending this house!" She sobbed and murmured, "Okay! Okay! I will! I promise!" And that was the end of that. I took a bath and went to bed. We never spoke about it again. She bore no visible signs of battle, no scars or open wounds, so next morning, we ate breakfast as though nothing had happened. You will find this strange, surely, but this was married life in America in the 1960s.

Now I see why you and your mother read so much. It makes you think, makes you see things you can't see, and that was my problem. I had all kinds of opinions, but I couldn't see a damn thing.

Things were quiet for a while. She stopped drinking, or so it seemed, and cooked and cleaned the way I thought a woman should. I must tell you that, during this period, I was in the streets doing my own thing. That, too, was a man's right. I'd come home after work, eat supper, hold you a moment, then head out. She'd ask where I was going, but after being ignored a few times, she stopped asking. I'd come home after midnight some nights, smelling like women's perfume. She'd cry in the morning, telling me she deserved better. I told her I wasn't sleeping with anyone, but she didn't believe me. If she couldn't go to school, she said, at least she wanted a family. I wanted one, too. But we were not saying the same thing.

DECEMBER 1ST, 2003

Dying is hard work. I spent most of yesterday vomiting blood and the little bit of food I'd eaten. My pajamas were stained, but I didn't have the strength to change or bathe. I just collapsed on the sofa and gasped until my breathing eased. Except for wanting to finish this, I'd have been happy to die right then. Yet since I asked Death for a little more time and she granted it, I feel compelled to finish what I started. If I can.

When you started walking, I knew you were different. So did your mother. She said she felt your difference in her womb. Said she knew you'd be special. That's why she protected you with all her might.

She really was wonderful except for her drinking. I look back now and wonder why she married a man like me. I guess we made the same error—allowing the world to define us. There weren't many other options in the '60s. Not for most black people. No other women in her family had a college degree, so, to me, her not achieving one was not traumatic. She lived to regret it and hated me for having interrupted her life's purpose, but I'd never even thought of college, so her not going hardly seemed significant. I knew of white people back home with college degrees, but no black people. Even our teachers hadn't gotten them. That wasn't a requirement for black country schools. So each time she broached the subject, I dismissed her.

Yet had she gone, she would've been extraordinary. She was smart as a whip. When she read to you, her voice sounded like music. She pronounced words carefully, as if handling something fragile. I never read to you because I didn't read well—not then—but I envied your mother's articulation. I'd listen to her repeat phrases into your eyes, and I'd be astonished that, over time, you'd repeat them back with perfect precision. She would've been an excellent teacher.

When you were in first grade, you told me and your mother you wanted to play the piano. We'd walked through Indian Springs Mall and passed a music store that advertised all sorts of instruments. A white man sat at a brand-new Wurlitzer, playing so beautifully you were hypnotized. I watched you, frozen with wonder, as you watched his fingers glide across the keys. I'd never seen you so taken, so enthralled. Rachel and I smiled and shook our heads. You stood there a long while, gawking with glee, until the guy lifted you onto the bench and let you bang a little. You struck arbitrary keys, but the man encouraged you anyway: "You're quite good, young man! All you need is a little practice!" You jumped from the bench, laughing and squirming. "I wanna play piano, Daddy! Can I?" I wondered what a brand-new piano cost, so I asked. Even the cheap ones weren't cheap! I knew I couldn't afford it, so I told you, "We'll see," and we left the store without talking any more about it.

At dinner that evening, you repeated, "Dad, I really wanna play the piano." I knew you and your mother had conspired because she never lifted her head.

"Is that right?" I mumbled.

"Yessir!"

I had no hesitation about you playing the piano; most musicians I knew were men. I simply had no idea how I'd pay for one.

"You know how much a piano costs, boy?"

You shook your head.

"Well, it's a lotta money."

We continued eating with our heads bowed. Your enthusiasm never waned.

"Fine. I'll look into it," I mumbled, sure that I was getting myself into something I'd regret. Your mother's smile relaxed my concern.

It took me over a year to save for that piano. I pinched nickels and dimes, here and there, and worked overtime many weekends to get it. I thought you had forgotten about it actually. Maybe you had.

Then, one day, you came home from school and there it was. It wasn't a baby grand, but it was a nice, shellacked, brown upright, and when you saw it, your mother said your mouth fell open and you screamed, "Momma! Dad got me a piano!" She said you touched it as if it were precious gold.

You tinkered with various keys as the sound lingered throughout the house.

When I got home, you met me at the front door.

"Dad! Dad! The piano's here!"

"Is it?" I teased playfully. "Where'd that come from?"

You hugged me tighter than you'd ever hugged me before.

"Now you gotta learn to play it, boy."

"I can already play a song!" you said and rushed to the instrument and fingered a simple melody.

"That's *pretty* good," I said, rubbing the top of your head, "but you need lessons so you can get *real* good."

You nodded and continued pressing keys until your mother sent you to bed.

"You did a good thing, Jacob," she whispered after kissing my cheek. "That boy might play in Carnegie Hall one day."

"He might," I said, "but I'll be satisfied if he just plays right here at home."

We went to bed in peace that night. She knew what I'd done to get that piano, and together we hoped it would change your life.

You started lessons with a woman down the street named Miss Lucille. You might not remember her because she moved away a year later. Then you went to a white lady your mother had heard about. I didn't like the idea, but Rachel said she was really good, and her color didn't matter. Soon you were able to play real songs, and, a year later, you were even better. I went to a few of your recitals—the only black man in the place—and I was proud. You really caught on fast. You started playing complex stuff, songs that sounded like classical music, and I told your mother she'd been right—you might indeed play in Carnegie Hall one day.

Well, something happened at the beginning of your third grade year. You approached us one evening after dinner and said you didn't want to play the piano anymore. Your mother and I exchanged frowns.

"What's wrong, baby?" she asked.

I didn't say anything yet. I simply sat up and planted my feet firmly on the floor.

"Nothin." You shrugged carelessly. "I just...don't wanna play anymore."

We knew you were lying. You chewed the inside of your jaw and shuffled your feet slightly, the way you always did when you were hiding something.

"That's not true," Rachel said. "You don't just decide, all of a sudden, to quit playing the piano. Not after all we've done for you to do it."

"I just don't wanna do it anymore, Momma. That's all."

It was your sass that ticked me off.

"Boy, you listen to me!" I stood. "I don't know who you think you talkin to or why you sayin any of this, but you got another thing comin if you think—"

"Okay! Wait a minute," your mother intervened. "Don't get upset, Jacob. Let's see if we can figure this out."

I huffed angrily.

"Just sit down and relax. We'll get to the bottom of this."

I sat, but my rage didn't subside.

"Kids are makin fun of me, Momma," you confessed. "They're saying mean things about me!"

You collapsed into your mother's bosom. I stilled my beating heart.

"Things like what?" she asked, but you never answered.

I already knew.

"Do I have to keep playin, Momma? Huh?" you murmured, staring deeply into her sympathetic eyes.

I responded before she could. "Do you know the money I paid for that thing? I don't care what else you do in life, but as God is my witness, you gon play that damn piano!"

"Jacob!"

"What? I don't care nothin bout his feelins! I don't care what kids say about him. He's gotta learn to stand up for himself. Or ignore them!"

Your mother didn't disagree; she just disliked my directness. Still, the bottom line was that you were going to play, whether you wanted to or not. I had sacrificed too much for you to throw the piano away that easily. So you dragged yourself to lessons for the next few years until, one evening, something remarkable occurred. I'll never forget it. I'd had a hard day at work—white supervisor breathing down my neck—and I would've quit except for you and your mother.

Anyway, I heard you playing when I came through the door. It was late, somewhere around nine, and I wondered why you were still up. I think you were preparing for a recital or something, so I didn't bother you. But I heard you. And whatever you were playing was the most beautiful thing I'd ever heard. I stopped and closed my eyes. The melody was slow and sad. The way you played it gave me chills. I hadn't realized you'd gotten that good. Perhaps I'd not been paying attention. Yet, in that moment, you sounded like a real concert pianist. I eased down the hall, next to the room where your mother had moved the piano, and I relaxed against the wall. You didn't know I was there. As I listened, your playing healed me.

I've spent a lifetime trying to remember that song, but I never could.

You had a gift far greater than anything I understood.

So I didn't interrupt you. Instead, I tiptoed away, resolved to continue doing whatever necessary to provide for my family. You stopped taking lessons a year later, but by then you were good enough to play anything. I never heard you play that song again.

After your ninth birthday, I began to force boy things upon you—and reading wasn't one of them. Your mother didn't agree, but she didn't fight me either. Sometimes she came along with us, to play ball in the park or whatever, but most times she didn't. Yet she never stopped reading to you. She simply did it when I wasn't around.

I tried to make you like football. I bought a whole uniform for you—jersey, pads, cleats, helmet—and still you resisted. You simply didn't like sports. But I didn't care. You were going to play because boys played. So every Saturday morning we went to the park and threw the football back and forth. Whenever you cried, I spanked you and made you get it together. I never really whooped you. Not the way Granddaddy had whooped me. Rachel wouldn't have had it. Plus, in Kansas City, you couldn't do that in public. Folks went to jail for that. So I spanked you and usually you'd straighten up. We even had fun a few times. I remember your laughter now. It was a heavy chortle, a sort of hollow rumble from deep within you. So I started tickling you simply to hear you laugh. I needed some assurance that you were a boy, a real boy, and that I wasn't a total failure as a father.

I hoped that by taking you to Kansas City Chiefs games you might grow to love sports, but you didn't. All you did was ask for your mother, but I reminded you that this was for men, so you stopped asking.

Since you didn't like football, I tried baseball. The results were the same—"Can Mommy come with us?"—and I fumed.

You tolerated it, but you didn't want to be there. You liked only the hot dogs. As long as you had a hot dog, you were fine. But the minute I urged you to study the game, to stop daydreaming, you became frustrated. Once, I grabbed your little biceps and shook you hard. You cried so badly we left.

When we got home, your mother was upset. "You can't make the boy into you, Jacob! He gotta be himself. Not all boys like sports. How bout asking him what he likes?" She frowned. "I know what you're trying to do, and it ain't bad, but you can't make him into you!"

You were going to play baseball if it was the last thing I did. I signed you up with a Little League and off you went. I knew you hated it. You didn't try to hide your feelings. But I at least wanted you to make friends with other boys on the team. There was a kid named Christopher who became your friend. I was happy about that. Do you remember him? Y'all spent the night with each other sometimes. He was a tough little boy. You'd pitch and he'd catch. His father and I sat on wooden bleachers, grinning like Cheshire cats. We predicted one of you might go to the major league. We weren't really serious, but it was fun to dream.

You played Little League baseball until around age eleven. I picked you up from practice one Saturday afternoon, and you asked, "Do I have to keep playing, Dad?" I stared through the windshield in silence. "I'll do it if you want me to, but I don't want to." What does a father say to that? I knew you hated it, but I couldn't let go of my hope. "Yes, I'd like you to keep playin. Does a boy good to be outside and active in something." I slapped your leg playfully; you looked away. I felt your torment, but it didn't move me. My distress hadn't moved Granddaddy either. I thought I was doing a good thing.

Eventually we stopped going to sports games. Well, I stopped taking you. Larry, Christopher's dad, and I went all the time. Usually we brought Chris along. He loved sports and loved watching them. I was jealous of how they shouted together in excitement or frustration. I was alone. I had a boy, but he wasn't with me. He was home with his mother, reading books.

That Christmas—I think it was 1974—I did something that probably scarred you forever.

It was around nine o'clock in the morning. I thought you'd gone back to sleep, since we'd been up opening gifts in the wee hours of the morning, but you hadn't. You were on the floor in your room with your back to the door, playing with toys. I stood, watching you, not with suspicion or judgment, but merely to witness your happiness. All was fine until you started talking to that doll. I remember it well. It wasn't a baby doll—you know I wouldn't have had that—but it was a *doll* nonetheless. Your mother and I had fought about it for weeks. She'd said there was no harm in you having action figures. They were soldiers and superheroes—those whose company I should approve. "They're still dolls," I said, although I gave in.

I couldn't hear what you said to them. It seemed innocent enough—until you lifted one to your face and kissed him. It wasn't sensual or anything; it was just the fact that you did it. I didn't know what you meant in your heart, and I didn't care. I shouted, "Isaac!" You turned abruptly, startled out of your mind, and leapt to your feet.

"I was just…um…doing what Mom does when I hurt myself. She kisses it and makes it feel better."

My panting increased. You tried to say more, but nothing calmed me.

"They're fighting, Dad, and he got hurt, so I kissed his eye to make him feel better." You shuffled anxiously, like a desperate toddler about to wet himself. You were too scared to cry.

"Give me that damn thing!" I said, and you laid it quickly in my trembling hand. Before my senses returned, I pulled the head from the body and tore the legs in opposite directions.

"I'm sorry, Dad! I'm so sorry. I didn't mean nothin by it. I was just doing what Mom—"

I pushed you down and screeched, "Boys don't kiss other boys in my house! Do you understand me?"

Your head never stopped nodding. Still, you didn't cry. I think that's the only thing that saved you. I hated when you cried, how you sounded pitiful and whiny. But you took the correction like a man. You gathered all the figures, as I directed, and took them to the trash.

Your mother's fury didn't move me. "We spent all that money on those toys, Jacob, and you gon make him throw them away?"

"Yes, I am. I don't want him playing with that shit anymore!"

We were silent the rest of the day. Your mother read a book, you did whatever you did in your bedroom, and I sat, like a stubborn stone, in the living room, staring into a cloudy winter day. I really thought I was doing the right thing.

DECEMBER 2ND, 2003

The only thing you really loved was school. Your mother had taught the prerequisites so well that you excelled with ease. Most children cry when parents drop them off for their first day, but according to your mother, you ran toward the building, bubbling with excitement.

It never crossed my mind to miss work to witness this milestone. I'd never known any man to do that. That was a mother's responsibility. To pack your lunch, comb your hair, stuff your satchel with pencils and paper. Buying the supplies was my job. When your mother asked if I were going to see you off in the morning, I frowned. She shook her head. I didn't understand. She didn't either. We'd come from very different worlds. Now we were finding it near impossible to live together. She'd read books; I'd tilled the soil. Her mind was far more developed than mine, but that didn't matter. I was still the man of the house, and she was supposed to follow me. That's what we'd believed. Both of us. At first.

As months passed and you grew older, she began to believe other things. The idea that a woman could be totally independent, unattached to a man, and, as Rachel put it one evening, "breathe her own air," made her eyes sparkle. I couldn't understand it. She was a reader—an avid reader—so I hardly knew her thoughts. She contemplated ideas and prospects years before they became important to me. One book, *The Feminine Mystique*, changed her life. She read it every night before bed and cried sometimes.

One day she murmured, "Women aren't slaves, you know." It was a casual statement, like one announcing the day's weather. I could tell she'd been drinking. "Nobody's a slave," I said, confused. "Yes, somebody is," she returned sadly. Her remark startled me, but I didn't entertain it. Years later, I thought about it and cried.

She worshipped that book like the Bible. It went with her everywhere she went. She talked to it as if words on the page were tongues of fire that cleansed her. I'd never read a book in my life. Not a whole book. And I had no interest in reading that one. I thought that perhaps this little book was planting seeds of rebellion in her head, so I warned her against it. She laughed as if I were stupid. Then, days later, I asked her to stop reading it altogether. "It's ruining our marriage," I said, "and making you hard to live with." Her eyes narrowed. "I gave up everything for you, Jacob Swinton. Everything. And now you want my mind, too?" I said nothing. "Well, you can't have it." She walked away, mumbling, and read that book every night until she finished it. When she did, I saw freedom dancing in her eyes. It scared the hell out of me.

She started volunteering at a women's shelter. I wouldn't have cared except that sometimes dinner was late. I confronted her one evening when she returned, and she said, "Cook your own dinner for a change!" Too stunned to react, I simply made a tuna sandwich and went to bed. She slept on the sofa that night, something she'd never done before.

She didn't touch me in those days; she didn't want to be touched. She wanted to be respected, and I didn't know how to do that. This might sound ridiculous to you, but it was true. Treating a woman as an equal wasn't even biblical, so I had no idea what it meant. It was inconceivable, really, laughable to the majority of America. Men *and* women. But your mother wasn't laughing.

I was still going out nights, spending time at bars and sports games. Your mother hired Jessica, the teenage girl next door, to watch you sometimes since both of us were often away. The idea of staying home at night with you while your mother did whatever she did at that shelter was crazy to me. Insulting. I'd been at work all day, and the least she could do, I thought, was raise my son. I provided every means for her to do so; I did my part. If she wasn't going to take care of you, neither was I. Not at night when I, like every other man, was supposed to be relaxing. She could do whatever she wanted, but she was not going to make a fool of me.

One evening, Jessica became ill and had to leave. Your mother was already gone, so I was left with you alone. I'd not been a TV watcher, but you were in a corner with a book, so I had to do something with my time. It was 1975. When I turned on the set, I saw Margaret Thatcher—the new leader of the British Conservative Party who, a few years later, would become prime minister of Britain. I was confused because I had never heard of a woman leader of a nation. And she had beaten a man! Crowds cheered all around her and news anchors spoke of the power of women voters. I wondered how her male opponent felt—crushed underfoot by a woman in public. *Who is her husband?* I asked myself.

I turned the channel. Nothing else caught my attention, so I got my Bible and began to read. I skipped words I didn't know and reread passages I'd heard before. I liked the story of Moses and Pharaoh and the parting of the Red Sea. It reminded me of black people's struggle in this country. Moses also reminded me of Malcolm X. His rhetoric, his courage, his bold demeanor. He told it like it was. I liked that about him.

Eventually, I found a rerun of *Soul Train*. Don Cornelius was in the middle of introducing Gladys Knight and the Pips, who I always liked, so I watched the rest of that episode. Just to tease you a bit, I got up and started dancing around. You laughed and laughed, and that inspired me to act sillier, so I did. You even got up and danced along, and together we had a lotta fun. You didn't know I could dance, and I hadn't heard your laughter in a long while. We made our own invisible soul train line and each of us danced until we got tired. We went to bed happy with each other that night.

DECEMBER 3RD, 2003

Black folks were now calling themselves "Afro-Americans," so eventually I joined in. We had been Niggas, Negroes, Coloreds, blacks, and so many other things. "Afro-American" sounded official, so I adopted it. I had an Afro, too, so the term made sense to me. So did your mother. Hers was high and wide, like the biggest you see in pictures of the era. She wore those large hoop earrings, strutting about Kansas City like an African queen, which, of course, she was, although I was too damn stupid to see it.

Once I started working at the post office, which was the best government job a black man could find, I became friends with a guy named Charlie Rhodes. He was the smartest dude I'd ever met, and to be honest I admired him. He knew something about every topic, especially black history, which I knew little about. His passion made others sit down and listen, and that's what we boys at work did.

There were four, sometimes five, of us who ate lunch together. We'd gather on fold-up chairs beneath a little tree behind the building on 58th and Prospect. Inevitably an argument arose, usually between Charlie and a guy we called Fats. It never went well for Fats.

"Y'all know King coulda been the first black president," Fats said one day out of the blue. "He was for the whole country."

Charlie shook his head and said, "Are you crazy, man? White folks ain't votin for no Nigga, don't care how nonviolent he is."

"They might. You never know. Plenty white folks marched with King when he was living."

"Course they did! That's how they do! They act like they standin with you until you get authority over them. Then they stab you in the back."

"Some Negroes do that, too!"

"They do! But they ain't got the power to alter your life. If white folks don't like you, they can mess up your whole damn existence."

I ate a fried bologna sandwich and a bag of Lay's barbeque potato chips as the exchange heated up. I knew *never* to open my mouth.

Fats added, "King was the best thing that ever happened to Colored people."

"You stupid as hell!" Charlie shouted. "I respect the man and all, but I ain't lettin nobody spit in my face while I just stand there, doin nothin. That's some bullshit, man!"

"No, it's not. He was tryin to make a point."

"And what was that point? That kissin white folks' asses gon make them love us?"

We all cackled.

"You see it didn't work, don't you? They ain't never stopped killin us. Hell, they killed *him*! They love when we talk non-violence. It means they go home alive while we bury each other."

"Man, you missin the point. King was tryin to say that you don't become like your enemy if you're trying to defeat him. Yeah, it cost us a lotta lives. That's true. But it changed America, didn't it?"

"Hell no, it didn't! We still dyin every damn day, man! Shit, police shoot us whenever they feel like it."

Fats didn't challenge that point.

"They kill us in a lotta other ways, too," Charlie said. "Ain't you heard of the Tuskegee syphilis experiment?"

Fats shook his head. I hung mine.

"Damn! Y'all gotta read, man," Charlie scolded. "That's what's wrong with black people. Too much shit we don't know."

He paused long enough for us to feel stupid.

"The American government started an experiment back in the '30s down in Tuskegee, Alabama, where they gave black men syphilis to see how it acts over time. The problem was that they didn't tell the men themselves. Nor did they provide medical treatment once the men found out. They coulda just gave 'em penicillin and cured 'em, but they didn't. They let 'em die."

"All of 'em?" I asked.

"Not all of 'em, but too many of 'em. Hell, one is too many."

We nodded.

"The only reason the experiment ended was because some white boy told on 'em."

"See! That's my point," Fats said. "Everybody white ain't bad."

"Aww, man! Give me a fuckin break," Charlie grumbled. "Just 'cause a few crackers do a few good things don't mean white folks ain't the problem."

"Yes it does! It proves that there are good people in every color. I know lots of white folks hate Colored people. I ain't no fool. But I know plenty Colored people who hate Colored people. And that's worse."

Charlie rolled his eyes. "Of course that's worse! But the reason black people hate black people is 'cause white people made us hate ourselves."

"Come on, man! That ain't nothin but an excuse. We can think for ourselves now. Slavery *been* over."

"No it ain't. Not in our minds. We didn't start this mess about light skin versus dark skin and all that shit. They started that. We just inherited it."

"But we can't be victims forever, Charlie. We gotta think for ourselves sometimes. Like you said, we can read now, so we can't blame white folks for the rest of eternity."

"I ain't blamin white folks. And I ain't no victim. I'm just tryin to explain why we are where we are."

Fats shook his head. "Where we are is our own fault."

"How?" Charlie screamed. "Huh? How? All we do is work

and make them rich while we stay poor. How is that our fault?"

"Because we don't stand together. That's our fault. We can't blame nobody for that but ourselves."

Charlie started pacing. "What! Are you crazy? Every time we stand together, they shoot us down! Ain't you ever read about the slave rebellions or Black Wall Street? Colored people been standing together since we got off that goddamn boat! That's the only way we've survived—by standing together."

Fats threw up his hands.

Charlie continued: "This what Malcolm was sayin!"

"Oh, don't start that again!" Fats cried. "He taught too much hate."

Charlie's lips trembled with rage. He set his sandwich down and closed his eyes.

"Awwww shit!" Stevie McLaughlin, one of the other guys who worked with us, murmured. This was getting out of hand.

Charlie looked at the sky and screeched, finally, "Mutha-fucka, is you crazy?"

Fats fought hard not to be intimidated, but he was fighting a losing battle.

"Malcolm was the most revolutionary leader black people ever had. Period!"

"Malcolm was not revolutionary! Yeah, he wanted black power, but how is that different from white power?"

Charlie's eyes bulged so large I thought they would pop from his head. "What the hell are you talkin about, man? Black power is not just the opposite of white power! It's black people's way of trying to get a piece of what we earned from this racist-ass country. We'd gladly share power—if white folks were willing. But they ain't! And that's the problem!"

"Some of them are. And that's enough. We gotta be willing to work with those who are. And move past the past."

"What the hell does 'move past the past' mean?" He mocked Fats's high, squeaky voice.

"It means we gotta stop talkin about slavery and lynchings and stuff like that and focus on today. I'm tired of hearin about all that old stuff."

Charlie froze. So did me and Steve. Looking Fats squarely in the eye, he said sincerely, "You bout the dumbest Nigga I know. It's black people like you who talk stupid shit like that and set us back every time we try to move forward." Anger shivered across his lips.

"Come on, Charlie," Steve said, "it ain't that serious. We all friends here."

"It *is* that serious, man! It is. That's the point. We sittin around bullshittin about our own future, and y'all don't even take it seriously."

"I take it seriously," Fats sassed, "but I don't live in the past."

"Don't nobody live in the past, man! The point of history is to tell you how to live in the future. So people don't make the same mistakes over and over."

"Now that makes sense," Fats said, although his words only inflamed Charlie further.

"How bout we talk again after you start readin some shit! Just don't say nothin else to me, man, until you spend some time with some knowledge!"

"I read all the time!" Fats declared, clearly offended.

Charlie shook his head violently. "No you don't! Ain't no damn way! You too stupid to read all the time. Ain't no way that's true!"

"You don't know what I do at home, man!"

Charlie threw up his hands. "Fine. Fuck it. I'm done!" He snatched his lunch pail from the ground and stomped away, shouting, "Y'all free to be as dumb as you like. All that fightin for the right to read, and now we won't even do it!" He shook his head as he marched toward the building. Before entering, he shouted over his shoulder, "Ain't that some shit?"

Usually we cackled after these exchanges, but not this time. Charlie's wrath had exposed all of us. Too much of what he'd said was true.

I spent days beating myself up for what I didn't know. I thought about going to a library, but I didn't. I wouldn't have known where to start. I even thought about buying some books from a bookstore, but I didn't do that either. I was drowning in ignorance and afraid of knowledge. No good to a living soul.

DECEMBER 5TH, 2003

By age twelve, you wanted to be an actor. Your mother told me one evening that you had earned the lead in a school play. Her pride bubbled over, so of course we went.

It just happened to be her thirty-first birthday. You must've been in the fifth or sixth grade. Most parents in the audience were white, but a few Afro-Americans sat scattered among them. Your mother and I took the first row. She squirmed with excitement. I was proud, too.

The play was *Little Orphan Andy*—an offshoot of *Little Orphan Annie*. Everything was fine until you burst forth in a fire-red wig, flinging your arms wide, bellowing, "'Tomorrow, tomorrow, I love you tomorrow! You're always a day away!'" I'd never been so embarrassed in my life. Slowly, I melted into the seat, wanting to snatch you from that stage. *Why did you let those white folks turn you into a clown? Don't you know boys don't prance around like that?* There were so many things I wanted to say. I escaped to the bathroom and remained outside. Your voice had been pitch-perfect, but I didn't care about that. I cared that you had made a fool of yourself.

Afterward, you and your mother exited, arm in arm, laughing loudly. You were in your element. I'd rarely seen you so happy, so proud. Rachel affirmed, "You were wonderful, baby! Just wonderful!"

Both of you froze when you saw me, smoking a cigarette, leaning upon the hood of the car. I suppose you assumed I had left, but I hadn't. I was hiding, trying to survive my shame. I couldn't figure out why your mother wasn't disturbed. Of course she liked whatever you liked. She simply wanted you to be yourself. I wanted that, too, but not if it meant being *like that*. I never told you, but other fathers shook their heads as I walked out. I saw them, whispering to wives and sons, declaring, "I would kill a boy o' mine if he did that."

All I could think about was what Bobby Joe or Charlie might've said. I wouldn't have survived it. They probably wouldn't have said anything, actually, just hung their heads and walked away. If they had asked, *How did you let your boy get like that?* I would've had no answer.

We should've gone to dinner to celebrate your mother's birthday, but instead I drove straight home. We rode in silence. I didn't look at you—you didn't look at me. You stared through the side glass, I stared through the windshield. Your mother studied both of us and shrugged.

"I won't participate in this," she murmured softly as we pulled into the driveway.

"In what?" I said.

"You know what. And you should be ashamed of yourself."

I scoffed and chuckled.

"He's just a child, Jacob. He's not a man yet, and he doesn't understand what you're saying to him."

"Yes, he does. He does! He's not a baby, Rachel. He's eleven years old, which is too old for that shit."

"Jacob!"

"Don't *Jacob* me!"

"First of all, he's twelve, and second of all, he'll learn—in time."

"It *is* time! Right now!"

You didn't say anything.

Your mother added, less confidently, "And he's learning, I'm sure."

"No, he's not. If he was, he wouldn't have done nothin like that."

Your mother's voice rose a bit. "He didn't do anything wrong! That's the part they gave him, so that's the part he played."

"And that's the problem!" I shouted. "He shoulda turned it down. Don't no Colored boy prance around like that in no damn red wig!"

"It's just a play, Jacob! My God!"

I slammed the gear shift into Park, causing your mother to screech.

"You don't get it, woman, 'cause you ain't no man!"

"No, I'm not a man," she declared, "but I know one when I see one."

I stared into her eyes. What was she trying to say?

"Let's finish this in the house, please. Isaac's tired and needs to get to bed. He has school in the morning."

I didn't move at first, but then I sighed and got out of the car. You two followed.

When we stepped through the door, Rachel said to me, "You should be glad your son is so talented, so admired by his peers, that he gets the lead in a school play."

"They used him!" I mumbled fiercely. "And he let them. Don't you see that? And he looked like—"

Your mother's narrowed eyes warned me to watch my words. I didn't finish that sentence. She would've had my head, and you would've burst into tears, so I kept that thought to myself. But I couldn't lie. All I could do was wonder how in the world to fix you.

Of course, you were already outside my reach. I was your father—*am* your father—and you were a stranger to me. Certainly I was selfish. I never asked how you felt about your performance, if you were proud of yourself, if you thought you sang well. I didn't want to know. My hope was that a good night's sleep might erase in my mind the horror of what you'd done.

It didn't. When I woke, you were still in my consciousness, dancing and prancing, tossing that red wig to and fro like a fool. My anger resurfaced, and you know what happened next. You haven't forgotten it; you couldn't have. I haven't either. It was the beginning of our end.

We sat at the little oval-shaped breakfast table your mother bought from the Swop and Shop out on 63rd Street. There were sunflowers in a vase at the center, and the morning light shone bright and warm through thin yellow curtains. I remember this because I dislike sunflowers. They look, to me, like weeds in bloom. And I've never been fond of yellow although it was your mother's favorite color. Anyway, the three of us took our places without greeting—you, before a bowl of Frosted Flakes, your mother and I before eggs over medium, potatoes and onions, and smoked bacon. Yet none of that saved us that morning. Rather, it didn't save me. We ate like prisoners in a mess hall—silent, heads down, accused. I smelled alcohol on your mother's breath, which intensified my frustration, but I didn't address that. My mind was on you.

Halfway through breakfast, I looked at you and asked, "Do you want to be a sissy, boy?"

Your mother stopped eating but didn't look up. Pain settled into your eyes. I can still see it. That should've been enough to cool my rage, but it wasn't. I repeated the question: "Do you wanna be a sissy, boy? Huh? Answer me!" You and your mother shared glances of pity and empathy. That only increased my anger. "I said answer me!" Your mouth cracked, but suddenly your mother said, "Don't say a word, baby. Never answer another man's disrespect."

She had humiliated me in front of you.

I slammed my fist upon the table and shouted, "Don't ever insult me in front of my son!" She stood, equally belligerent, though far more elegant, and bellowed, "Don't ever insult my son!" You were crying now. Your mother and I were eye to eye, waiting for someone to make the next move. I turned to you. "Answer me!" You only wept harder. "He's fine, Jacob," your mother insisted. "There's nothing wrong with him. Nothing he needs to explain to you." She was a mother bear, protecting her cub. Well, I was a grizzly who didn't intend to back down. And there *was* something wrong with you, something you needed to explain to me, and I meant for you to do it. So I grabbed your collar and yanked you to your feet. "You will answer me when I ask you a question, boy, do you understand?" You nodded once or twice, but still didn't speak. Your mother had turned, and, in a flash, held a butcher knife to my throat.

She was clear, calm, and resolved. "Let. Him. Go," she whispered. Your body hung limp from my fist. I relaxed it and you collapsed to the floor like a corpse. Rachel and I never broke our gaze. She instructed you to go to the bathroom to clean your face—all while staring at me. I fully believed that, had I moved or opened my mouth, she would've stabbed me. I had no doubt of that.

She lowered the knife eventually and told me to have a good day. My eyes bulged. She smiled, cleared the table, and it was over. Just like that. I stared, frozen with disbelief. There was nothing more to say. I had been dethroned.

You went to school, presumably, like any other day, and your mother went about business as usual. At work that morning I dreamed so many things. Like sitting your mother down, in your presence, and reprimanding her for having overstepped her boundaries. But that wouldn't have worked. She'd been reading those books and working at that shelter, so she didn't have the mind of submission.

I thought of whipping her again but decided against it. It was you who stopped me. You adored her. I knew that. And any physical aggression toward her would've ruined you. Or ruined what you thought of me. And although I was not proud of you, I still hoped, somewhere in my mind, to shape you into the son I wanted. No woman would deny me that. The other idea I had was to take you from her completely.

She had drinking issues, as you know, and any court in the land would've chastised a drunk mother. I could've done that, but again you would've hated me, so there would've been no victory.

Our home became a tomb. No one said a word. You did homework and read books, as usual, in the corner of your room, as if afraid to move about the house. Your mother and I ignored each other completely. We sat before the TV without acknowledging each other's presence. I felt she owed me an apology; surely she felt the same. Neither of us relented. We endured a week of hell. In bed, we were careful not to touch. She faced one direction, I faced the other. I had vowed never to be relegated to a sofa in my life—not by a woman—and I've kept that vow.

A week later, we eased back into our fractured life. But there was no way to mend it. In the mornings, she'd play sleep until I showered and left, then presumably she'd rise and do the same.

You rarely lifted your head during those days. I didn't think much about it then. I think about it all the time now.

Your mother broke silence on Good Friday. She said at breakfast, "I want us to go to church Sunday. We're a family and we ought to be together on Easter." I nodded.

The sermon was awful. All the preacher said was, "He got up!" We laughed and mocked him as we ate dinner together that afternoon. The laughter felt good.

DECEMBER 7TH, 2003

Your mother and I stopped touching altogether. She lost all desire for me; I got tired of begging her. So I went to others for my physical needs. It was unspoken, but it was not unknown. Your mother certainly knew. She warned me simply to *keep that in the streets. Bring no piece of it into my house.* I respected that. Perhaps she had someone, too. I never asked. I doubted it though. Women were criticized for such behavior back then, and your mother was nothing if not publicly upstanding. Even her alcoholism—a term we didn't use yet—was masked with great discretion whenever we left home. No, if she'd had someone I would've known. At least I think I would've. There would've been hours for which she could not account, and I don't remember that. I thought that perhaps her claim of spending time at the women's shelter might prove false, so I followed her several times and watched her enter and exit the place, and always she came straight home afterward.

I met a woman in the late '70s whom I liked very much. She wasn't your mother—beautiful, graceful, poised—but she was *easy*—something your mother wasn't. I do not mean sexually available or without personal standards; I mean uncomplicated. I could talk to her without filtering my words. She didn't ask where I'd been if she hadn't seen me in a while. And she never asked for money. I liked that. We were not in love. We were in need of things spouses couldn't provide.

I sometimes wondered, though I didn't ask, if my lady friend loved her husband. Our personal lives were off-limits. However, she spoke occasionally of a son who had died shortly after birth. His name was Reuben. Whenever she mentioned him, she brimmed with tears. He was perfectly healthy, she said, but one morning she woke, and he was dead. No one knew what happened. Even doctors were baffled. I assumed she was married because she had a baby. Any respectable woman in my day would've been. In hindsight, it was probably SIDS, but doctors didn't know about that yet. We agreed, she and I, that God simply wanted him back. But if that was true, she pondered, why did God send him in the first place? I had no answer.

She announced, late one night, that she was pregnant. She was afraid, she said, but she told me not to worry. *I'll handle it.* I knew what that meant. I didn't agree with it, but I had no other solution. Now that I am old, I've considered that perhaps she raised the child with her husband and never said anything more about it. We stopped seeing each other after that, so she could've done it. Perhaps it wasn't even mine.

It certainly could've been, but I had no idea who else she might've been seeing. I didn't press the matter. She'd implied I was the father, so I didn't refute her. She was a lovely woman who wasn't a liar.

I'm telling you this because you might have a sibling somewhere in the world. I know this is crazy, but you deserve to know. There is no honor in this admission. I've thought about the child every day. I've run through my brain every scenario conceivable. *Perhaps she wasn't pregnant at all. Perhaps she lost the child. Perhaps it was born prematurely and died. Perhaps she died somehow before giving birth.* But most likely, she got rid of it. Or raised it with another man. I don't know.

Her name was Leah. Leah Campbell. I suppose it still is, unless she's married someone else, which I doubt. I never knew where she lived, but she worked at that famous diner down on Independence Avenue. Maybe they have records, a paper trail you could follow. If you want to know. If you don't, I understand. This might be more than you care to bear at this point in your life, but it also might be just the thing you need. Again, it's up to you.

Leah might be dead by now, but she was younger than me. The child would be an adult, ten or twelve years your junior. I'd wanted you to have a legitimate sibling, but it never happened. Your mother conceived several times, but never carried full-term. We agreed, after the fourth failure, to stop trying. Or so I thought.

I came in late one night, smelling like smoke and perfume, and your mother accosted me at the door. "This is a family," she said, "and it takes both of us to keep it." I didn't know what she was talking about, so I dismissed the comment and proceeded toward the bedroom.

Her next words startled me: "And if you think I'd have another child with you, you must be a fool."

I blinked and turned. "What did you say?"

Her voice rose slightly: "I'm not having any more children, Jacob. I don't want any more. Not with you."

Was I hearing right? What exactly was she saying?

"You got something to say to me, woman, you say it!" I shouted, angrier than I'd intended.

Her eyes blazed: "Why do you think we haven't had more children? Huh? Why?"

I didn't know what to say.

"Because I didn't want any more! That's why! I took care of it every time!"

You took care of what? my narrow eyes asked. She panted heavily, realizing, finally, the magnitude of her words. I collapsed into a nearby chair; your mother stared at the floor. Suddenly she clasped her mouth and cried. My eyes glazed, but I didn't weep. There was no sound in the room. Only a painful stillness that left us unable to speak or move.

She'd killed our babies? That's how I saw it. And I knew I would never forgive her.

Once the shock lifted, I whispered, "I'm done."

She didn't protest. It wouldn't have mattered anyway. No black man during that time could have heard this and not been broken. White folks argued about abortion, but most black people were clear: *YOU DON'T DO THAT! GOD DECIDES WHO LIVES AND DIES!*

I couldn't even look at her. I felt as if I didn't know her at all. She wiped her face and shuffled into the bedroom. I sat in that chair, all night long, wondering what children had come but never arrived. The more I thought about it, the more hurt I became. Hurt is worse than anger, you know. Anger dwells in the head, then fades. Hurt lingers in the soul. It rearranges your feelings without your permission. It blinds you. The only other time I'd felt this way was the day Esau died.

Next morning, she tried to apologize, but I wouldn't hear it. Nothing she said eased my bitterness. I let her talk, but I can't recall one thing she said. I was done and she knew it. "It doesn't have to be this way," she insisted, over and again, but in my mind, I was already gone.

It hit me that perhaps that book had made her do it. Maybe someone at the women's shelter had read it, too, and convinced her to follow its instructions. What else could it be? Something had to justify her decision, something outside the world in which we lived, and I needed to know what it was.

I bought a copy of *The Feminine Mystique* and began reading it. I had never read a whole book in my life, and I had no intention of reading all of this one, but I wanted to read enough to discover the source of Rachel's betrayal. Page one captured me. The chapter was titled "The Problem That Has No Name." Yes, that's what I was looking for—your mother's problem, her indescribable difficulties that made her do such an unforgivable thing. But that's not what I found. What I found was the claim that everyone in society, for their own personal gain, had used women. The author said that women had cleaned the house, cooked, ironed, driven kids to school, and served their husbands at night, but wanted more. I frowned. What more was there? Wasn't this her job?

The husband had a job, too. Liking it wasn't a requirement. I huffed and shook my head. Yes, this damn book was at least partially responsible for Rachel's actions.

Days later, I threw it away. It didn't matter anymore. I was done with your mother, so I moved out. I was thirty-four, thirty-five, something like that. Your mother stopped me at the door and said, "You think this is my fault, but it isn't. You'll realize that one day. I may be dead and gone, but you'll see it. I promise." She nodded confidently, but I frowned and walked on.

I moved into an apartment on 23rd and Brooklyn Ave. It wasn't really an apartment, more like a room with a bathroom and tiny kitchen area. It was far in the back of a widow's house, in the basement in fact, and no one in the world knew I was there. At first, I liked that, but then as time wore on, I found myself completely alone, and I hated it. Loneliness can kill you, you know. It makes you think and do strange, unhealthy things.

Still, I tried to make the place home. I bought a little plant and set it in the window above the kitchen sink. I looked at it every day and sometimes spoke to it as if it might speak back. Many days, it was the only comfort I encountered. The day it bloomed, I stared in surprise and wonder. It was life. Beauty. Happiness. The white petals of the peace lily gave me hope that I'd survive. I had a TV, but no books. No curtains, no dishes, no towel sets, no matching bedsheets or comforters— nothing that makes a house a home. In fact, I don't think I ever opened the windows. It was dark in there most of the time, regardless of the hour, and that's exactly how I felt. The best thing I ever did was move out of that black hole. But, for a while, it was home.

DECEMBER 10TH, 2003

Your mother and I were complete strangers now, moving in opposite directions. My one concern was you. A boy needs a daddy, I believed. I believe that still. He needs a momma, too, but his father's presence is not optional. I committed, within myself, to seeing you every evening after work. My new place was only ten or fifteen minutes away, so that wasn't a problem. And I kept that promise pretty well. Do you remember this? All those evenings I watched you do homework. I wasn't much help because I wasn't an academic, but I was there. Sometimes, when there was no homework, we'd watch TV or sit around talking. But I was there. That's when I told you about your great-granddaddy Abraham and your uncle Esau and hard times in Arkansas. You seemed only semi-interested, but I didn't expect more. I simply wanted you to know your inheritance.

"You have land in Arkansas," I told you. "Lots of it."

That piqued your interest. "How much?" you asked.

"A little over three hundred acres."

"How did we get it?"

Your curiosity inspired me. "Your great-great-grandfather Wilson Swinton came from Africa on a slave ship. It docked in Charleston, South Carolina. He and his brother Peter were captured together, we believe, but sold separately. They both remained in South Carolina somewhere. When slavery ended, Wilson heard that the government was giving free land to anyone willing to move west. So after a while, he and his wife, Chaney, gathered their six children and headed out. Some-one told them money grew on trees in a place called Arkan-sas, so they went there. A white man stopped them midstate and sold them five hundred acres of bottomland near the Ar-kansas River."

You sat up straighter, intrigued, and asked, "I thought the land was supposed to have been free?"

"It was. They lied. Your folks knew better than to trust white folks. They'd dealt with them their whole lives. They'd saved money over the five or ten years since slavery ended, doing all kinds of things."

"Like what?"

"Well, folks said Chaney was a hell of a seamstress. Said she could make a dress out of rags better than any sold in a store. Her mistress had loaned her out sometimes to other white folks for weddings and stuff like that, and she saved a quarter here, a dollar there, if they gave her anything. Many times, she didn't get nothin. Wilson, her husband, broke mules. Everybody used mules for farming back then, so he was al-ways workin somewhere for somebody. He put his money with Chaney's, and they left. Some said Wilson traded gold for cash, too."

"Where did he get gold from?"

I paused and smiled. "Africa."

Your eyes beamed. I had no idea you cared about any of this, but in hindsight, it made sense. You were a reader; you lived in your imagination.

Subconsciously, I moved to the edge of my seat and continued: "When they were captured and brought over, some smuggled gold in their mouths and butt cheeks. They saw how white folks valued it, and our people hoped it would be useful wherever they were going. According to the story, Peter gave his portion to his brother Wilson, your great-great-grandfather, who hid it and kept it safe until freedom came. I guess the gold plus the money they had saved was enough to buy the five hundred acres the white man offered. They settled there, in a little community called Blackwell, and that's where I was raised."

"Why is there only three hundred acres now?"

"Because during the Great Depression they sold two hundred to make ends meet. I always wanted to buy it back, to keep the inheritance whole, but I was never able to do it."

We talked more than we'd ever talked before. Do you remember this? You loved the story, the details, the particularities of our history. I loved that you loved it. So I told you everything.

"Wilson and Chaney's children, the ones I heard of, were Matthew, Jessie, Cordelia, Josephine, Ruthie Jean, Anthony, Charles, and Abraham."

You shouted, "That's my great-grandpa, right?"

"That's right. He was the baby."

You squirmed on the sofa and folded your legs. I think you felt connected to something larger than yourself. I hope you remember this.

You then asked, "What happened when they got to Arkansas?"

I said, "The Swintons built a mansion deep in the woods. You couldn't have stumbled upon it. You either knew how to get there or you didn't. They liked it that way. They were quiet, unassuming people who never bothered anybody. They could go days without talking at all. To anyone. Even each other. Can you imagine that? A house full of people who say nothing at all for days. That was the Swintons. They were unlearned, but resourceful. Their main occupations were mule breaking and fur trapping. Wilson brought the knowledge of mules from South Carolina and taught his boys how to do it. They all became masters. They weren't rich, but they weren't sharecroppers either. His daughters caught game and skinned them alive. Those girls were as tough as any boy around, people said. They could wrestle a half-grown calf to the ground in seconds. Wilson taught them to set traps in the woods and shave fur so clean the animal could've put it back on and walked away."

"Daddy!" You doubled over with laughter.

"That's what folks said! They were creative, hardworking people," I emphasized. "They didn't play. And they didn't trust education. They had no way of verifying what teachers taught, so they avoided formal schooling altogether. None of them could read, but they could count. You couldn't cheat them out of their money. That was for sure. And they made plenty of it. They usually ate the animals they skinned, so food was generally plentiful, and since mules were the tractors of the day, they were always in business. They were modest people who didn't believe in fancy things like expensive clothes and appliances and lavish furniture."

Your big brown eyes sparkled. "Did you know any of Grandpa Abraham's brothers and sisters?"

I shook my head. "They all died before I was born."

You sulked, but I chuckled and continued: "One of the girls got mauled by a bobcat one night, and Wilson and Chaney rushed her to the hospital in Morrilton. They didn't take Colored patients back then, but they took her. Rumor had it that Wilson extended a wad of bills so thick he could hardly hold it in his hand. White doctors operated and saved the child's life. Days later, she had a limp, but she was alive. That was enough for them. She ended up birthing nine children. I think her name was Cordelia."

We talked late into the night. You loved the story. Your interest thrilled me and made me proud to be a Swinton. Before heading to bed, you asked, "Are you gonna watch *Roots*, Dad? My teachers said we should."

Charlie had mentioned it at work. They'd been previewing it for weeks on TV, and truthfully I'd sorta been looking forward to it. So I half smiled and said, "Yeah. I guess I will."

"Me, too!" you screeched joyfully. "Especially now!"

I smiled as you disappeared into your room.

I came by the house every evening and watched each episode with you. It was early 1977. Your mother couldn't take much of it, but you and I saw it all. It was the first depiction of Africa I'd ever seen on TV. I didn't know how much you

knew, since you were a reader and all, but I was totally unaware of anything concerning black people before slavery.
I felt ignorant; I *was* ignorant. I hated the way white folks
treated our people. You did, too. I saw it in your eyes. While
the Wrestler instructed Kunta Kinte in the hull of the slave
ship, I wanted to grab you and hold you and never let you go.

I cried when they beat Kunta Kinte for refusing to give
up his name. I hadn't meant to. Tears welled suddenly, and I
couldn't hold them. I imagined you leaning upon the whipping post, declaring your name for dear life, and water burst
from my eyes. Surely you remember this. No son forgets his
father's tears. They come rarely in a lifetime. You turned and
stared at me softly, sympathetically. I saw love in your eyes.
You looked as if you wanted to hug me, but you knew better.

Your mother gave me a tissue and touched my shoulder lovingly. This was our first physical contact since I'd moved out.
I realized how much I missed her. And needed her. You cried,
too, but that was no surprise. You were freer in your spirit
than me, which, of course, I resented. Everything moved your
heart, and I mean *everything*. You cried in church, you cried
from falling, you cried when your mother cried, you cried at
romantic movies, you cried from disappointment, you cried
with joy. I suppose you cried about me.

One episode of *Roots* featured Chicken George, Kunta
Kinte's grandson, who trained fighting cocks. We sat on the
sofa, you and I, at opposite ends but closer than usual. Midway through the program, you asked, "If Chicken George
is the master's son, how is he a slave?" I said, "Because his
momma, Kizzy, is." And you said, "But shouldn't he be free
if his father is?" And I said, "Everybody oughta be free, son,"

but I hadn't answered your question. Truth was, I didn't know anything about the legal status of slave children. That troubled my mind. As we watched Chicken George travel about, making good money fighting roosters, you asked, "He don't get to keep nothin, Daddy? Not even a little bit? He's doing all the work!" I nodded but remained silent. *Roots* was angering me in a way I couldn't explain. I knew black labor had built America, but I didn't know how black pride had been stripped from our flesh in the process. We had worked, hundreds of years, for absolutely nothing. I couldn't conceive of that. It was like going to a job every day, but never getting paid. I sighed with rage. You asked if I was okay, and I said yes, but I wasn't. I could've killed a white man right then. But I held my peace in order to enjoy our time together.

By week's end, you had asked a thousand questions about slavery and black people I couldn't answer. I felt stupid. But more importantly, we had seen, for the first time, the story of a black family on national television. And they weren't buffoons or clowns. We ate popcorn and drank soda every evening as if sitting at the movies. On the last night, when Kunta Kinte's descendants finally left the plantation and journeyed to their own land in Tennessee, you shed a few tears and said, "They bought land, too, Daddy. Just like Grandpa Wilson." I was proud of the comparison, proud you remembered. You said you wanted to trace our family tree and I told you I'd help. You asked if I would take you to Arkansas. I said of course. So we went.

DECEMBER 11TH, 2003

It was the summer after your fourteenth birthday. I picked you up one Saturday morning at 5:30 a.m. You were asleep, so I practically dragged you and a brown paper bag of clothes to the car and headed up Prospect Avenue to Hwy 71 south. It was dark, only a few cars dotted the road. I heard, somewhere in my spirit, Granddaddy and Grandma and Esau beckoning us onward, calling us home. You woke around 10:00 a.m., looking around in every direction. I smiled at your innocence, your wonder, and asked if you were hungry. You shook your head and asked where we were. I said Alma, Arkansas. You found it on the map, then nodded. "We're almost there, huh?" you asked. I smiled and said, "Yessir. It won't be long now."

Your interest in the journey pleased me. The first time we drove to Arkansas, when you were only a toddler, you slept the whole way, waking only to eat and use the restroom. But this trip was different. You were thinking about our family story, I believed, wondering if it was true. *Roots* had inspired something in you, and you couldn't wait to feel the land, our land, beneath your feet. That's what I thought. And I was right. You started asking all sorts of questions: *Do black people live in Alma? Are there still segregated schools in the South? Are Kunta Kinte's descendants still alive? What happened to the big mansion Wilson and Chaney built deep in the woods? Do you have a picture of Uncle Esau or Grandpa?* I hope you remember this. It would kill me if you don't.

We turned left toward home. I slowed to a snail's pace. You sat up high, looking around in awe and wonder. "Is this it? Is this our land?" I shook my head. "Naw. Ours is on the other side of those woods there." You stared across a sea of green and almost yelped. I chuckled.

Then suddenly, I gasped. I saw Elliott Strong in your eyes. It was the same longing, the same soft, lingering pleading I beheld that awful day. I almost told you about him then, but I didn't want to ruin our trip, so I shuddered and dismissed the thought. "Is there a library close by?" you shouted. I shook my head. "Son, I've never seen a library in my life." Which was true. I'd seen the outside of one, but never the inside. "Where do kids go to school around here?" you asked. I frowned. I didn't know. Our black school, which had taught first through seventh grades, was gone—someone burned it down—and once I moved away, I never heard about the in-tegrated elementary school. "It's in town, I guess. Seven miles away. A place called Morrilton." You nodded, satisfied. Only then did I realize how much things had changed since I'd left.

We made another turn, off the main road, onto a dirt path. You squealed with pleasure. "Is this our land?"

"Not yet, Isaac. We're almost there. Hold your peace, young man!" You giggled and fidgeted as if you had to pee. I'd never seen you so excited—not about anything concerning me. I was overjoyed. This was part of my dream: you and me back home together, happy. The way a father and son *should* be.

Finally, we made the last left turn and there it was—home. The old house stood feebly, bent and frail, like an elder upon a walking cane. "That's where I grew up, son. In that little shack right there." I parked the car and we got out.

"You lived in *that*?"

"Sure did. It was a strong little house back when Grand-daddy and other men first built it."

"They built it themselves?"

"Men did that in those days. We did all our own labor."

You looked around at the trees and open fields, then back at me. "This is all ours, Daddy?"

"Yep. This is ours. This is what your grandpa Wilson bought when he brought his family from South Carolina."

"It's big!"

"You ain't seen nothin yet!"

I'd hoped, all my life, to bring a son back to the land, and there we were.

You walked toward the woods, so I followed. I warned of snakes, and although you nodded, I could tell you didn't really believe you'd see one. I took you to the spot where the mansion once rested and you were disappointed to find nothing but high grass and an old rusty, deteriorated wagon. You asked if that belonged to Grandpa Wilson, and I said, "Yes it did. That's how the family traveled to town and church." Truth was, I didn't know whose wagon it was, but I wanted to feed your anticipation, so I told you what you wanted to hear. We walked deeper into the woods until you froze and pointed, whispering, "Daddy! Look!" It was a deer and her fawn. I nodded and said, "Plenty of those round here. Mighty good eatin, too." You scowled. "That's how we survived, son. We lived off the land. We ate wildlife, grew our own vegetables, drank well water, washed clothes in the river. That was our way of life." You shook your head. "I couldn't eat that deer," you said. I chuckled. "Oh, you would've eaten it—or starved to death." You didn't like those options, so you shrugged and moved on.

Everything amazed you: butterflies, turtles, hawks, squirrels, wild turkey—a whole flock of 'em—rabbits, frogs, lizards. You had never seen any of this in the wild. I boasted that, as a young boy your age, I could run a rabbit down and catch it with my hands. "Really, Daddy?" you asked with disbelief. "Hell yeah!" I squealed although I'd never done any such thing. It sounded like something a country boy ought to be able to do, so I said it. We rested atop a fallen tree trunk as I bragged about other feats, too: I said I could carry two square bales of hay, one in each hand, all the way from the field to the barn, nonstop. I said I could grab a snake at the throat before it could bite my hand. I said I could swim from one side of the river to the other totally underwater. Each tale left you astonished. These lies seemed appropriate under the circumstances.

It was hot that day, though somewhat cool in the woods. Everything was green and in full bloom. You asked if I knew the different types of trees, and I told them to you. I explained that most houses back in the day were made of cedar, and you asked why, and I said because termites don't eat cedar. Then I took the leaves of an oak, a cedar, a mulberry, and a birch tree and showed you the differences. You liked that kind of knowledge. Actually, you loved any kind of knowledge.

We resumed walking until reaching the river. It had obviously rained recently because rushing muddy water practically overflowed its banks.

"Me and Granddaddy fished this river *a many day*," I said, staring into the golden flow.

You frowned and repeated the phrase, "A many day," trying to figure out its meaning.

I chuckled playfully and rubbed your head. "During the summer, it got so low we could walk straight across it."

You seemed unable to imagine that. "What kind of fish did y'all catch out of here?"

I said, "Crappie, bream, catfish, perch, drum, gar, buffalo."

"Buffalo?" you screeched. "I've never heard of a buffalo fish."

"Most people probably haven't. It's large with a small, round mouth. It's thick and meaty, too, sorta gritty tasting. Many people don't like it, but if you fry it hard, it's okay."

You asked if I could skip rocks, and I said, "What? You kiddin me? When I was your age, I was the rock-skippin master!" You laughed as I searched for smooth, flat stones with which to prove myself. "It's all about the angle," I said. "You gotta get the angle right or the stone'll sink." I flung a stone, with the flip of my wrist, and it skipped five times. "Oh wee, Dad!" you screamed. "That was good! Teach me how to do it!" I gave you a stone, stood behind you, and guided your hand with my hand. We looked like complementary shadows, moving together in the art of stone skipping. We had rarely been that close, flesh to flesh, since you were a baby, but now you were a teenager, and things felt awkward. I noticed how much you had grown. Your head reached my chin, and for the second time I imagined you as a man. The thought frightened me. You might recall that I dropped your wrist suddenly and moved away. You scowled, but I acted oblivious. I was so insecure! What father can't touch his own son?

You cast a stone and it sank immediately out of sight. "Try again," I said, standing slightly apart from you. You grabbed another rock and tried to mimic my form and method but failed once again. Frustrated and disappointed, you kicked loose soil and murmured, "Aw man!" I had ruined the moment and didn't know how to fix it. Touching you had left me uneasy. You tried again and again, but all your efforts proved futile, so we left.

Walking home was pretty intense until I began to speak of our family history again. That's when your mood lightened.

The trip was perfect—except for your mother's absence. You asked if she had seen the land, and I said sort of. She'd certainly been there, but she hadn't been so far into the woods. When I first met her, I told you, she stayed with your aunt Loretha, meaning she wasn't allowed to accompany me into the woods. No decent girl would've done that back in my day. Out of nowhere, you asked, "Why did y'all divorce, Daddy?" The question caught me off guard. My first inclination was to remind you that you were a child who had no business asking such things, but instead I relaxed and spoke to you like a man: "Your mother did something unforgivable." You frowned a bit and asked if you could ask me something else, and I said go ahead. "Have *you* ever done something unforgivable?" You didn't look at me. You recoiled, afraid I might strike you. I'd made you so timid, so fearful of me. I reached to touch your shoulder, but you winced and squeezed your eyes shut.

I never answered your question that day, but I never forgot it either. This letter is my answer.

DECEMBER 13TH, 2003

We arrived back at the old house, and I drove you to the community cemetery, behind the church. You read the name aloud as we entered: Rose of Sharon. The pencil-thin path was narrow and weeded, just as it had been in mule and wagon days. I warned, once again, of ticks and chiggers, which you had never had, but would hate by morning. Time slowed as we walked, ushering us into another dimension. At each tombstone, I told you the story of the people: who they were, how we were related to them, the role they served at the church, how they died. So many had died young. Fevers, polio, accidents. Life was hard for black children back then. We worked like adults. We were beaten by our parents for the slightest offenses. We feared whites more than we feared God. We suffered cuts and bruises without medicine. Many children lived, but just as many died. You shook your head. I told you that, unlike us poor country kids, you lived a life of royalty. No black child I had ever known had had his own bedroom. Or three pair of shoes. Or enough clothes to change every day of the week. Or choices of what to eat. Or choices period. You smirked with shame.

We moved about until standing before a huge gray headstone with large, black letters that read HENRY and BILLIE JEAN MOORE.

"Who were they?" you asked. "And why is their stone so big?"

I smiled and said, "They were the wealthiest black family in Blackwell. They were light-skinned people, almost white, with thick, curly, good hair. But they were black. Mr. Henry, as we called him, was a tall, stocky man who worked as the dean at Philander Smith College in Little Rock. He was so smart even white folks tipped their hats at him. But he wasn't uppity. He was actually a kind, friendly man. His mother, Miss Eloise, was low sick for a long time—several years—so Mr. Henry never went far although he could've. He had eight brothers and sisters, and lost all of 'em before finishing high school. I don't know how they died. One drowned, I remember hearing. But after so much tragedy, he and his mother became really close. Folks said he was the sharpest pencil in the drawer, meaning the smartest of his siblings, and I'm sure they were right. I can't imagine anyone smarter. He was the Sunday school teacher my entire life, so any real knowledge of the Bible I possess, I attribute to him. He was strict and stern, but not mean. We understood the difference back then."

His home sat upon a small hill in a meadow of flowers. It was something from a fairy tale. As children, we'd been forbidden to enter it. I always wondered why until realizing, as an adult, that folks didn't want our black hands to soil a precious thing. Mr. Henry's mother died one breezy, fall afternoon, and a week later, he and Miss Billie Jean moved to Little Rock. That pretty mansion deteriorated over the years, crumbling slowly as if in continuous mourning.

You asked where our folks were buried, and when I showed you, you sighed. There were no massive marble tombstones with fancy letters or expensive artificial flowers framing the graves. Our folks had refused to *put good money in the ground*, as they said. There was only an aluminum plate with barely legible names to mark their resting place. It was as if they were merely thrown in the ground and covered up, you said. Esau's mound had no headstone at all. I knew where he lay because I was there when they lowered him into the ground. A small bunch of jonquils bloomed just above him the next spring and every year thereafter. In April or May, I'd go, misty-eyed, and stand over my brother and remember our times together. The day I left Arkansas, I promised to buy a headstone for his grave, but I never did.

Suddenly, you fell to the earth and, like a shaman, anointed Esau's resting place. "Hey, Uncle Esau," you said. "This is your nephew, Isaac. So nice to meet you." Your small, tender hands grazed the entire grassy mound. Then you stood.

Guilt and grief consumed me. I stared at the grave and apologized silently. I think I wiped my eyes a few times, if I recall. You reached for my hand, but I didn't surrender it. I just stood there. I wanted to hold your hand, needed to hold your hand, but I couldn't.

You cried, although I didn't understand why.

Years later, I realized it was for me.

At Granddaddy's grave you did the same. You looked like a healer. Your connection to the dead seemed very real. You sensed things. It would be years before I understood this gift in you. I didn't know anything about spirituality during those years. I knew a little about religion, since I'd been raised in the church, but religion didn't help me that day. So I watched you and prayed that you weren't doing anything against the Word of God.

Truth is, you've always felt things and responded to people's emotions. I'd never heard of anyone talking to dead people before. Well, that's not true. We had people in the community down home who claimed to hear dead folks and could pass messages on to the living. I guess we believed it because we feared it. I just never gave it much thought. But when I saw you that day, moving and moaning in trance, I knew you possessed something neither of us actually understood. Eventually, you sighed and smiled as if returning from a faraway place. I stared at you, wondering who in the world you were.

From Granddaddy you turned to Grandma and started praying in an unknown tongue. That's when I really got scared. Yet minutes later you calmed and said, "She's still hurting, Daddy. I can feel it." I told you to stop it. This was not a game. You said, "I'm not playing a game, sir." I heard the seriousness in your voice. You hung your head and wept as if you'd known her, as if you could hear her pleas. I'd never seen anything like it. So peculiar yet so real. At one point, you doubled over with pain that wasn't yours. All I could do was stare at you as you sobbed. Soon, you stood, brushed dirt from your knees, and said in someone else's heavy baritone,

"She's fine now. We can go whenever you're ready." I studied you intensely; none of this made sense to me.

As we began to leave, you suddenly closed your eyes and said, "Who else is here, Daddy?" I ignored you and insisted we go. You obeyed, but maintained, "Someone else is here. I feel them." I began walking down the grassy lane toward the car. You followed but didn't want to leave. "Who is it, Daddy?" you kept asking, but I wouldn't answer. I couldn't. Not yet. It wasn't time.

DECEMBER 14TH, 2003

We returned to Kansas City just as we'd come—you asleep most of the way, me driving and thinking about things. Anytime I went home to Arkansas, I returned sad and pensive. I loved that place. What it did for me, how it made me the man I am. Well, the man I *was*. That land, that precious black soil, transformed my sweat into an inheritance I was proud of.

You were my boy, and you had trod where I had trod. You had walked the same earth as Wilson and Chaney Swinton, and thrown rocks into the same river as Esau and me. You had been inducted into a lineage of strong black men because you were my son. There was no greater joy.

If I could do things over, I'd raise you on the land. It's what I knew, where my beliefs made sense. You wouldn't think ideas have geographical context, but they do. We teach certain things because of where we live. We like to think we're

governed by some higher spiritual or philosophical motiva-
tion, but really most of our thinking comes from our envi-
ronment. Granddaddy used to say, "A man ought to live by
the sweat of his brow," which is certainly an honorable thing,
but this applies more to the farmer than to the executive. The
businessman definitely endures difficult, strenuous labor, but
it doesn't necessarily produce sweat. Granddaddy had no notion of that life. So he taught what he knew—as we all do—
and tossed around proverbs that promised one's success with
the soil. I should've stayed. Or at least returned. I might've
been a decent father on the land. You might've been proud
of me. Yet there was no hope for me in the city. Everything
was new, different, evolving, and I couldn't keep up.

Many black people left the land in search of an easier life.
The swap wasn't worth it. We got to big cities and realized
we had less than we'd had before. The land was our hope,
our guarantee that we wouldn't starve. Once we left it, our
lives were up for grabs. Cities devoured us whole. Drugs,
unemployment, crime all took their share as we shook our
heads at what we'd left behind. Now, most black kids across
the nation have no connection to the soil at all. Their people
escaped the country, believing they were escaping a life of
toil. I understand that. I did that myself. But we lost the gam-
ble, I'm afraid. It's sad that so many black kids have never *felt*
the earth, never let mud seep through their toes or planted a
seed then watched it grow. This, I believe, is a spiritual loss.
The ways of God are more obvious in the country. We left
the land, and white folks gobbled it up and created estates for
their children while, in big cities, we scrambled to pay rent
or mortgages on half acres of nothing. Whatsoever you do,

Isaac, keep the land. If you have no heirs, find some deserving black child and give it to him. He'll thank you for it one day. We all will.

DECEMBER 17TH, 2003

First snow fell yesterday. It came easy and unannounced, like a whisper, but once it started, it continued into the night. When I looked out this morning, everything was still, white, and gleaming. I wondered if you were somewhere safe and warm. I wondered if you were thinking about me.

After we returned from Arkansas, things were good for a while. I helped you create a family tree for your history project, and you wrote a story that went along with it. You added a bit about our trip home although you didn't mention your experience at the cemetery. I was happy about that. You got an A on the project, and your mother and I took you to Gates and Sons Barbeque. That's what you liked, so that's where we went. She'd been drinking pretty heavily that day, but she insisted we do *something* to celebrate. You ordered a pulled beef sandwich and fries, and your mother and I shared a slab of ribs. I see it all in my head now. It's funny what you remember in old age. Memories reveal who you used to be, what you once thought important, what regrets you cannot shake.

Do you remember the incident with the napkin? You unfolded it as if it were a delicate thing and laid it across your lap. Then you lifted it and dabbed the corners of your mouth. I snatched it from you and screeched, "Men don't do that! Women do that!" I think it was the fact that we were in public that embarrassed me. Before I stopped shouting, your mother slapped the shit out of me.

I trembled from the shock and the sting. People looked at me with pity and shame. Your head dropped, almost to the table, and your mother, with wicked eyes, dared me to touch you again. I would've hit her back had we been at home. Yet men who hit women in public were weak and good-for-nothing.

Things went silent for a moment, then the craziest thing happened: two black women approached our booth. One of them said to your mother, "Sista, sista. Please don't do that again. It's not right and it's not your place to humiliate your man in public." Your mother gawked. "Mind your business," she said, angrily, but they persisted. "It's women like you," the other added, "who run good men away from home. No man deserves to be belittled in front of his own son, much less the world." I agreed, but your mother didn't. "Get you a man before you tell me how to keep mine!" she shrieked and threw a plastic cup at them. That's when they dispersed. You and I stared at each other. She'd never been so distraught, so undone in public. She grabbed her purse and ran out.

I followed. "Leave me alone!" she bellowed, fumbling

through the parking lot. I hesitated, but didn't leave. She was crying silently. Anger wrinkled her forehead and twisted her mouth. She collapsed behind the restaurant dumpster and wept fully. It was a terrible sight, seeing her slumped over that way. I reached to comfort her, but she shoved my arms away, so I stood calmly until she relaxed and sat up. "Just leave," she huffed, exasperated. "Take Isaac home. Don't let him see me this way." I turned to go. "And never step foot in my house again."

I almost said it was *my* house since I was paying for it, but I remained silent. She didn't mean what she'd said anyway. I knew that. I took you home and told you to get a bath and go to bed. I never knew how your mother got home that night.

Weeks later, she called and asked if we could speak about you.

We sat, once again, at the little oval dinette table. Neither of you said a word when I entered. You didn't even look up. I knew something was wrong. In her usual sweet voice, she said, "Isaac's sick, Jacob. He needs help." I looked at you but saw only the crown of your head. Your mother continued: "Tell your father what you told me." She was obviously upset, which shocked me a great deal. I'd never seen her upset with you. Not seriously. "Tell him," she murmured slowly. You peeked upward and shook your head. I had no reaction because I had no idea what was going on. "What's the problem?" I asked. Your mother stood abruptly but refused to speak for you. Like me, she stared at the top of your small, round head and waited. "What's the matter, boy?" I asked a bit more forcefully.

Finally, you raised your head and mumbled, "I think I'm... different, Daddy. That's all."

"Different how?"

"You know how!" Rachel shouted.

"Mom!" you cried, but she ignored you. Again, I was surprised. She'd always protected you, fought for you, argued for your right to be you, but not now. And her disappointment broke your heart. I saw the pain in your eyes, and I felt for you. You'd never wailed like that. You'd cried many times, but not like that. You'd obviously thought she'd take your side, but when she didn't, you didn't know what to do. I didn't either. So I stared at both of you with stark confusion. I wasn't surprised. You'd never mentioned a girl before. And I'd seen no signs that you wanted manhood. So your confession only solidified what, deep in my heart, I already knew.

Your mother's reaction was surprising. It seemed she'd never considered this. I couldn't understand why. There was nothing particularly boy-like about you, and that had always been true. Yet maybe, in her mind, the two things—a boy's softness and his urges—had nothing to do with each other. I disagreed. I thought one was the sign of the other. Anyway, she demanded I do something. "Do what?" I asked, startled. She couldn't say, but she didn't want some *sick child* in her house. That's the phrase she used. I hope this doesn't upset you. You know she didn't mean it. She never loved anyone like she loved you. But she wanted you to have a family of your own one day, and she couldn't see that happening if you were *that way*. I'm sure she wouldn't care now, but then she was very disturbed. Hopefully, you've buried all of this and moved on. I mean only to reveal how we, your mother and

I, were sometimes complicit in your heartache. Perhaps you don't even remember it, but I think you do. Hurt is hard to forget, especially from a mother. And healing is never easy for black men.

Rachel paced nervously, irritated that I didn't share her frustration. It made no sense to me, her burning fury, when I'd been the only one asking you to be something else, something more masculine, all those years. I'd thought she was fine with you being *you*—whatever that meant—and that in her eyes, my desire to change you had, in fact, been insensitive and downright offensive. Now I saw that she wanted a *free* son, yes, but not a *different* one. She wanted a son the way every mother wants a son. She'd dreamed a life for you just as I had. And neither of us would get what we dreamed.

"Do something, Jacob!" she repeated. "You're his daddy!" but there was nothing for me to do—except swallow the truth that I'd failed as a father. It must've been true. That was the only logical explanation. I should've kept those ugly thoughts away from you, but I hadn't. A good father steers his son in the right direction and protects him from sick, sinful things. I had not done that. I didn't know how. Lord knows I'd wanted to! Staring at the top of your head, I wished I had been harder on you. I should've made you stick with baseball when I allowed you to quit. I should've yanked you from that stage when you pranced about in that ridiculous red wig. I should've dragged you to Chiefs games when you preferred your mother's company at home. That's what a good father would've done. Yes, your condition was all my fault. A boy becomes whatever his father allows. Your mother apparently agreed: she looked to me to fix you, to say something that would make you right, but I had nothing to say.

We sat at the table for hours. Your mother asked endless questions about how you'd become what you were. You provided no answers. Several times you screamed, "I don't know, Mom! Okay? I don't know!" But she bellowed, "You do know! You do! No one ends up like this without knowing how! When did it start? When did you decide to be this way?" Nothing you said satisfied her. She probed endlessly until I insisted she stop.

"I won't stop!" she declared. "Not until—"

"You will stop," I demanded, "and you'll stop now."

She conceded, shaking her head. I told you to go to your room. You eased from the chair and shuffled down the hallway. When your bedroom door closed, I reached for your mother's hand, but she withheld it.

"What are we going to do?" she asked matter-of-factly.

"We?" I screeched. "We who?"

"You and I. Us."

"I don't know. I tried years ago, but you stopped me."

"I didn't stop you! I just didn't want you to hurt him."

"I wasn't hurting him, Rachel! He's a boy! I was trying to raise a man, but you couldn't see that. I guess you do now." I paused and sighed. "If anyone's to blame, it's you."

"Me?"

"Yes, you. You fought me every step of the way! You said I was too hard on him, so I let up." I shrugged and lifted my hands.

"When did you ever listen to me? Huh?"

I cackled with sarcasm. "Rachel, you can't blame me for

this. You can't. You undermined everything I tried to do. Even when I whipped him—"

"You whip a mule, Jacob! Not a child. I didn't want you to beat the boy so badly he hated you."

"I didn't care if he hated me! He woulda been *a boy*, Rachel, and that was the point. I didn't need a friend!"

We continued until tiring out. She regretted calling you sick. She told me this later; I'm sure she told you, too. Your truth was simply more than she could bear.

I walked to your room and squeezed the knob tightly but didn't enter. Somewhere in my heart, I hoped that perhaps you would change and decide to be normal. But who was I fooling? I let the knob go, closed my eyes, and accepted, finally, that I couldn't change you. You were beyond me, beyond my control, and I didn't know what to do with you. I didn't know what to do with my feelings about you. I turned and left. I went home, sat in the dark, and smoked the night away. I wished Granddaddy or Esau had come and told me what to do, how to survive this, but they didn't. I was on my own this time.

The next day, I waited for you after school. You were almost fifteen by then. I parked a few blocks away and leaned against the car until you burst through the exit, chatting with friends. When you saw me, you froze and stared. I said nothing, made no gestures, but you moved toward me anyway. I dropped a cigarette and smashed it into the pavement, then returned to the driver's side and got in. You opened the passenger door carefully, like one afraid to awaken a sleeping giant, and eased into place. We pulled away without greeting.

I stared forward; you stared through the passenger window. It was a cool autumn day. Orange, red, and yellow leaves swirled about. My first words were something about the beauty of the season. Then I asked about your day, and you said it was all right. I nodded and tried to think of other things to say, but nothing came, so once again we rode in silence all the way into Kansas, far down State Avenue. I wondered what your mother had said to you the previous night, but I didn't ask. Your nervous disposition made me uncomfortable. We ended up in the parking lot of Oak Ridge Baptist Church.

I silenced the engine. Before I could speak, you huffed and said, "I'm fine, Dad. Really. I shouldn't have said that to you and Mom yesterday. I'm okay." At first, I didn't believe you. I told you not to lie, but you assured me you were telling the truth. You said you'd been confused because you weren't like other boys. You didn't like sports or fighting. You loved reading and singing and dancing. I told you that that was okay. Men did that, too. You nodded. I smiled and touched your shoulder. My eyes watered with relief.

My error was wanting to believe you, needing to believe you.

"Be the kind of man *you are*," I emphasized, "but *be a man!*"

"Yessir," you said. "I will. I am. I'm sorry. I was just…um… confused. But trust me—I'm fine." I rejoiced. We laughed and chatted about all manner of foolishness, then went, once again, to Gates and Sons for barbeque beef sandwiches and fountain Pepsis. You were *not* funny after all. I'd feared, the day before, that if you were, I would have no legacy. That you'd have no wife, no children, no way to carry our name into the future, which meant our family was doomed. I'd thought of Granddaddy and Esau. How could our family end just like that? All because you were something you weren't supposed to be? It didn't make sense, so I'd prayed against it. I'd asked God to change you, to put girls into your heart, and when, in the church parking lot, you said you weren't *that way*, I praised God for having answered my prayer.

DECEMBER 18TH, 2003

My clearest and most painful memory is the time your mother called the police on me. You were fifteen.

I was at the house fixing something your mother had asked me to repair. I don't recall what it was. You and Rachel had just returned from shopping. I asked, "Where y'all been?" and you retorted, with a snarling sort of tone, "We were just out." I looked at you with disbelief. *Who the hell are you talking to?* I wondered. Your mother gave you a look. She saw my anger and warned, "Don't get beside yourself, Jacob. He didn't mean anything by that." You added, "You should come with us sometimes if you wanna know where we go." Your mother cleared her throat quickly. You frowned, unsure of the weight of your words, but clear that you'd said something wrong. I leapt over a chair and brought you down with one blow. "You will respect me in my house!" I shouted with each strike. Your mother tried to pull me off you, but my rage was immovable. "Stop it, Jacob! Stop it! He didn't mean it that way!" But I didn't care how you'd meant it. It was the fact that you'd said it at all. You had no right to talk to me that way, to suggest how I should manage my time.

Eventually, my anger calmed, and I panted heavily. Your mother was shouting into the phone, but I paid her no mind. I think she called for your uncle Tyree first. I heard her shout his name, but they must've been unable to find him. Then, frantically, she dialed another number and took a more formal tone. That's how I knew she had called the police.

You lay on your side on the kitchen floor, a slight trickle of blood streaming from the corner of your mouth. Your mother slammed the receiver on the base and helped you to your feet, all the while rebuking me for my outrageous behavior. Her words I can't recall because I didn't hear them. I heard only the sound of her voice, protesting and reprimanding me from afar. Suddenly, winded and appeased, I collapsed in the same chair I had surmounted as the room began to swirl about me. Within moments, the doorbell rang, and two white policemen entered.

"What seems to be the trouble, ma'am?" one asked your mother while frowning and staring at me. She hesitated, undoubtedly second-guessing her decision to call them, but she had to say something: "He was beating my son, and I feared he'd hurt him, but he didn't. We're okay now."

The bold one stood over me like a slave driver, and I cringed. I knew better than to speak. I bit my bottom lip and said nothing. "You done calmed down now, boy?" he asked me.

I studied the floor to steady my wrath. Had I moved or

opened my mouth I would've attacked him, and he would've killed me. So I kept my head down, praying they'd leave before my self-control expired.

The other officer approached you, sitting at the kitchen table with a napkin pressed against the corner of your mouth. He lifted your face with one hand and removed the napkin with the other. Seeing you weren't hurt seriously, he told his partner, "He's all right."

The partner told me, "Best control yourself, boy, 'less you wanna go downtown with us. And I don't think you do."

Staring hatred into his eyes, I thought, *Fuck you, you redneck son of a bitch!* but I didn't say it. I was mad, but not crazy.

When the police left, your mother ushered you to the bathroom and cleaned your face. She murmured something to you I couldn't discern, but I could guess: *Don't say anything tonight. Just go to bed. We'll talk about it in the morning.* Or something like that. You went to your room and slammed the door. Rachel returned to the living room.

"You didn't have no right to beat the boy like that!"

"He didn't have no right to disrespect me," I mumbled defensively.

"Disrespect you? Are you serious? He's a kid, Jacob. Even if he was wrong, you could've corrected him some other way. What the hell's wrong with you?"

I didn't answer.

"How can he respect you when you treat him so bad?" She paused a moment, then said, finally, "He'll never forgive you for this. Never."

I sat in that chair all night long, staring at the same spot on the floor. Too embarrassed to raise my head, I never noticed when your mother turned off the lights, bolted the front door, and went to bed. In the dark, I saw Grandma, standing beside me, shaking her head. What could I say? Yes, you had insulted me, but why had I reacted so violently? Maybe I wanted your place in your mother's heart. I'd dwelled there once. She'd adored me until you came, then everything I did displeased her. A few months after your birth, I began to miss the light that once sparkled in her eyes for me. It had been replaced with something murky, cloudy, and insincere—the look people give when they've given up on you. I thought that maybe she was tired and overwhelmed with new motherly duties, but the glimmer never returned. Not for me. I should've known then that we were done, but I kept hoping. Perhaps now I had accepted, finally, that she belonged to you—and you alone—and the realization devastated me.

Later that day, you approached the front door as I pulled into the driveway. Your steps quickened, it seemed, when you heard my car door open. I knew you wanted nothing to do with me, but I had to try. You were my only son. We couldn't live like that forever. At least I couldn't.

"Hey, Isaac," I called, "hold on a minute."

You paused, clutching the doorknob firmly, but did not turn. A step beneath you on the front porch, I hesitated, struggling to gather my nerve. There were no perfect words, so I said simply, "I didn't mean to hurt you."

You didn't move.

"I just...lost it." This sounded pitiful, even to me. "But a man shouldn't be disrespected in his own house."

You nodded slowly.

"Still, I shouldn't've done that to you. I was wrong."

You waited a second, then proceeded into the house without saying a word.

DECEMBER 19TH, 2003

Days passed before you even looked at me. I came by every evening, hoping to talk and clear the air, but you ignored me completely. If I remember correctly, you broke the strike only because you needed money for a canvas for art class. I gave it gladly and you said *thank you* merely out of duty. It was a start, so I took advantage of it.

"What are you planning to paint?"

You shrugged and said, "I don't know. It has to be pastoral though. That's what the teacher said."

"What does that mean?"

You sighed and rolled your eyes slightly. "It has to be a natural landscape. A painting of something in nature."

I nodded much too enthusiastically, then said, "I'd like to see it when you finish."

"Okay."

You shoved the dollar bills into your rear pocket and walked away quickly. It was awkward, but it was the best we—or rather, I—could do at the time.

I don't recall if you and your mother spoke much during those painful days, but you probably did. The few times I joined you for dinner, you glanced at each other and made eyes as usual. It was a strange thing, sitting next to people you love but being unable to love them.

I waited for one of you to yield, but you didn't. So one evening, I came by and met you and Rachel on the front stoop. "I don't live here anymore," I said, "but long as I pay the bills, I'm still the man of this family, and I don't intend to be disrespected." You and Rachel glanced at each other, then stared in opposite directions. "Now that don't excuse what I did. I didn't have no business actin like that. It was childish and beneath me." Neither of you responded. I suppose you had nothing to say, so I continued: "Ain't no need in us actin like this, all quiet and all. We still a family. We gotta work this out."

I was proud of myself, although there was no healing between us. In my heart, I felt free. I had taken the high road, I told myself, and if you and your mother couldn't forgive me, that was fine. I was no longer to blame.

I had made mistakes, yes, but I wasn't a total failure. I had worked too hard, sacrificed too much, paid too many bills to be a complete failure. So I never apologized. But by not doing so, I became what I feared. That's what I discovered during those dark days. Pride really can kill a man. Actually, it makes him kill himself. He justifies his errors and creates his own righteousness in his mind. Grandma used to say, "There is a way that seemeth right unto a man, but the end thereof is death." It's true. Men of my day were right because we said we were right. Our word was law and everyone else had to follow it or be punished. I couldn't understand why you and your mother struggled so fiercely against me. I gave you everything I had, everything you could possibly need, and still you seemed unsatisfied. In some ways, after the police incident, I quit trying.

We eventually resumed our lives, but things were not good. You asked for stuff you needed, spoke when you had to, said happy birthday on my birthday, but other than that, you hardly interacted with me at all. I was no better. But I didn't think I needed to be.

The fissure between your mother and me was too wide, too deep to mend. We drifted further and further apart. There was little hope for us. Except in you. You were the glue that held us together.

Remember the night of your art exhibition? I went with hopes of trying to mend things with you. I didn't care much for art really, but I cared for you, and I wanted things better between us.

When I entered the high school gymnasium, my ignorance immediately surfaced. People spoke in whispers, as if the art itself might hear and be offended. I heard words I'd never heard before, like *aesthetic* and *impressionism* and *surrealism*. I kept my mouth closed so no one would know just how dumb I was. Still, I saw many portraits I liked. One featured a black family—man, woman, boy, and girl—hidden among a forest of trees. Their bodies were shaped like trees, their eyes barely visible in the background. In fact, if one didn't look carefully, one could easily have missed the people altogether. It was dark, the picture, composed mostly of browns, blues, and blacks. The eyes, lingering in the dark, were like miniature fireflies lighting a midnight sky. I stood before this picture a long while, admiring some young person's enormous imagination. Several viewers commented that they, too, liked this picture and wondered how such a tender mind had conceived something so nuanced, so beautifully captivating. Whoever this child was, he or she would be wealthy one day, we agreed. I would've purchased that painting if it had been for sale.

Strolling along, I found other portraits confusing or downright ugly. Until I saw yours. Countless parents and students stood before it, gawking and frowning with awe. I approached, unaware that your picture was the subject of their admiration, so I prepared to see something good, something, perhaps, comparable to the earlier picture I had admired. Yet when I beheld the image, I stumbled slightly. A friendly man, the only one of two I saw all evening, grabbed my arm and asked if I was okay. I nodded and smiled, struggling to regain complete composure. My breathing returned, but in inconsistent whiffs, leaving me panting as if I'd been running. Sweat broke across my forehead, and a nice old lady, someone's grandmother surely, passed me a wrinkled napkin from her pocketbook, and said sweetly, pointing to the canvas, "Your boy?" I nodded. "You must be proud." I nodded again. "He's obviously something special. What a gift!"

Standing before me, in all its glory, was a portrait of my past—our land in Arkansas. The rendering was so exact I shivered. From every direction people commented: *It looks alive! Wow, so real, so full of life! I've never seen anything so marvelous! Who painted this masterpiece?* And on until I had to look away to stabilize my heart.

It was the most remarkable image I'd ever seen. Everything was precisely as we'd beheld it: trees, the old house, the open field, the clear, sea-blue sky. Within minutes, a huge crowd assembled, marveling that someone your age had such extraordinary perception. I could've boasted that you were my boy, my brilliant, artistic son, but I didn't. I didn't say anything because my voice wouldn't work. I covered my mouth and trembled. That same grandmother, touching me lightly, murmured, "You have every right to be proud." She patted my back several times. "Every right. Don't feel ashamed." But I *was* ashamed. Here I was, on the verge of emotional collapse, all because of a picture you had painted.

Eventually, you and your mother made your way through the crowd and beamed with satisfaction. She glowed as if you were receiving the Nobel Prize. You hid slightly behind her, obviously pleased that your work had solicited such immense criticism. Both of you looked at me and smiled, and I smiled back. It took everything in me not to burst into tears. I hated that my heart moved so easily, but I prided myself in the ability to control it that night. People congratulated me as if I'd done the painting myself. I quickly objected, "Oh no, no. I had nothing to do with this. He gets his creative side from his mother!" They chuckled kindly.

You won the competition, of course. Viewers moved on, but I stood there, hypnotized by your landscape and your indescribable talent. I think the fact that you had painted it at all, that you had remembered our time together, made me happier than I'd been in a long time. I was proud of you that day. I shook your hand firmly, if you recall, and said, right in front of everyone, "That's the best damn picture I've ever seen, boy. You shonuff got a gift!"

I should've said more. Should've hugged you freely and rubbed your head. Or something. You asked, "You really like it, Dad?"

I nodded, quite vigorously I remember, and nudged you playfully. Your mother said later that we looked like father and son that night. We'd never favored in her estimation, but in that moment, she said, we looked just alike. This was her dream: you being yourself while she and I celebrated. The picture took me back, of course, to our time at the cemetery, and I remembered you sensing the pain of our people. You had a way of feeling things that went beyond what I could comprehend. The name you assigned the painting only weakened me further: *Down Home.*

That landscape really was a masterpiece. And you are the most talented person I've ever known.

DECEMBER 21ST, 2003

Shortly after that, you started courting—that's the term we used in my day—a nice, pretty, light-brown-skinned girl named Marie. Do you remember her? She was shy but sweet, and your mother and I liked her. You didn't really date or go out—after all, you were only fifteen—but your mother and I spoke of you as a couple. We even thought of her as a daughter. You met up at school dances and the picture show sometimes. She said her parents thought the world of you, and my chest swelled with pride. I never met them, but I dreamed of sharing grandkids with them. Your mother and I didn't speak of your sexuality again. Marie was enough to assuage our worries. We teased you about her incessantly, and, on any given day, if you failed to mention her, we voluntarily reinserted her into our lives.

This paradise lasted a good while. Eventually, Marie vanished, but Vanessa appeared. I didn't really care for her

although your mother liked her quite a bit. She was tall—
five-ten or so—and lanky. She was far more masculine than
you, but as long as she was a girl—and she looked like a girl—
I registered no real objection. One evening when I stopped
by after work, you said, "Dad, I need to ask you something
personal."

"Sure," I said, and we escaped to the front steps. I had a
feeling it was about girls. I wanted it to be about girls.

You stood at the far edge of the steps, I stood somewhere
near the middle. "What's up?" I asked anxiously.

You cackled. "Be patient, Dad. This is hard enough already."

I smiled and waited.

"Vanessa asked if she could...um...taste me."

My eyes bulged; I laughed into the sky.

"What's so funny?"

"Boy, you got a lot to learn." I slapped your arm playfully.

"What am I supposed to say? She's not supposed to ask
that, right?"

My mouth opened wide. "You say, 'Hell yeah!' That's what
you say!"

You didn't find my response the least bit amusing.

"Listen, boy—anytime a woman wants to do that, you let
her. That's how she shows you she likes you."

You shook your head. Obviously, the act disgusted you, and
you didn't want to do it. Yet my joy couldn't be contained.

"Shit, boy, when I was your age, I would've given anything
for a girl to do that for me. I probably wouldn't have respected
her much, but those weren't the girls we married anyway."

"Well, what if I wanna marry Vanessa?"

I scowled and said, "You don't. You're too young to be thinking about that anyway. Enjoy these years. You'll never get them back."

Privately, I hoped you'd return to Marie, but I didn't say that. I was just glad you were a boy, having a boy's experience. I didn't really care about much else.

Vanessa disappeared shortly after that. I was relieved. Once, when I came over, your mother told me to stop getting so involved in your affairs, and I followed her advice. You brought home some other girl the day after your sixteenth birthday, but I don't recall her name. She wasn't pretty enough for you, I thought, so I didn't bother remembering her. But you liked her. You liked her a lot.

I picked you up from the movie theater one night, and you asked, "How old should you be before you have sex?"

I shrugged. "I don't know."

"Am I too young, you think?"

The idea of you having sex, especially with a girl, excited me far beyond any wisdom I had about it. "I think you're old enough," I said, although had you been a regular boy, I would've advised you to wait and share the moment with the love of your life.

"How old were you?"

The question caught me off guard. I almost shared the truth—that your mother was my first—but my inexperience felt like failure, so I said, "Sixteen."

"Who was the girl?"

I coughed, buying a little time, then said, "Her name was Josephine."

"Was she pretty?"

"I guess so. In country terms. Only a few girls were knockouts, and they weren't puttin out."

You laughed so hard your head fell between your knees. "*Puttin out?* Is that what y'all called it?"

I chuckled, too. "Yeah. That's how we described a girl's willingness. Boys were always ready—girls were always hesitant. They had far more to lose. Most just downright refused."

"But not Josephine?"

"Well, she wasn't sure at first, but I was pretty persistent."

"You were *that* charming, Dad?"

"Hell yeah, I was *that* charming!" I teased. "I told her it would feel good and we'd be in love afterward. She was tough to convince, but eventually she gave in."

"Did you love her?"

"Naw. I just wanted to know what sex felt like."

We snickered like adolescent boys.

"Did you like it?"

"Shit, yeah, I liked it! Every boy likes it!"

"What if I don't like it?"

"Ain't no such thing. A man is made to like it. That's what makes him go after it. It makes the world go round."

You asked, "Is there a right way to do it?"

"Yessir. There's a right way to do anything." I paused.

"Well, what is it?"

"Why you so anxious," I teased, loving every minute of this.

You squirmed a bit and I was thrilled. "'Cause I wanna know how to do it right—just in case. You know what I mean?"

"Yeah, I know." I paused again, then continued as the

sex expert: "You go real slow. That's the key. Don't rush a woman. She's already nervous and unsure, so you gotta make her comfortable and let her know she's safe with you. Don't *make* her do anything. Talk her through it."

You wanted to ask more specific things, I think, but decided against it. This was as vulnerable as we'd ever been. I didn't volunteer anything more because I didn't know anything more. Of course I'd had sex with your mother, but if I'd done it right or not, I wasn't sure. Where you'd learn the correct way I didn't know. Folks back home believed that nature told a man what to do, so I went along with that. It wasn't true, of course, but I was far too modest to say more. And you wouldn't dare have asked. So we skipped the particulars, and you inquired, "What did Josephine say afterward?"

"Nothin. She asked me not to tell."

"Did you?"

"Of course!"

We laughed together again.

"All boys told."

What I didn't say, what I should've said, is that most of us lied.

"Were you scared? To do it, I mean?"

"Naw, not really. Boys had talked so much about it that I couldn't wait to see what it was like."

"What was it like?"

I'd never tried to describe sex before. "It's hard to say, but it's damn good! A man and woman can't be no closer'n that."

I knew I was being vague, but it's the best I could offer under the circumstances.

"We don't need no babies though. That's the only thing about it. You can get more than you bargain for."

"Oh, I'd use a condom if I do anything."

I'd heard of those, although I'd never used one.

"Just be careful, whatsoever you do."

You nodded easily.

"A woman is not a toy. She doesn't like to be played with."

You said, "Yessir. I'll remember that."

My own contradictions aside, I thought I was giving you sound advice. Actually, I hoped you *would* have sex and want to tell me about it. I was convinced you'd never think of boys again if you did. We drove around for hours, laughing and talking my fears away.

DECEMBER 22ND, 2003

Then, during your junior year, girls stopped coming. I asked several times if you were seeing anyone and you said, "something like that," which I took to mean yes, so I remained hopeful. Your mother said I'd soured you from bringing girls home, so I apologized for having come on too strong. You smirked and said, "No, Dad. You're fine. I'll let you know if I get serious about anyone else." I smiled and waited. Weeks and weeks I waited. But no one came.

You were practically an adult now. Hair under your arms, small wild whiskers on your chin, nicely defined pecs and biceps. You looked like a young man. I boasted of you at work. I told the fellas you played basketball and were quite good at it, and they believed me. They had sons, too, some of them, and they shared similar stories of athletic achievement in their boys. I should've felt bad for lying, but I didn't.

I just wanted a son to brag about. That's a father's right, I believed. I believe it still.

But our lies—yours or mine—didn't last. You came home one evening with a tall, muscular young man named Ricky. Ricky Stanton. He appeared innocent enough and bore beauty I couldn't deny. I knew you shared something special because of the way he looked at you. There was desire in his eyes. He tried to blink it away, to look like a regular football star, but that yearning is hard to disguise. And I saw it. I didn't worry though, because you had dated girls, and I'd convinced myself that your years of confusion were over.

Ricky started coming home with you often. Your mother mentioned it to me, but not for concern. She was glad, she said, that you had a friend, someone you could hang out with. You were almost his height—six feet or so—and every bit as handsome. I teased both of you about girls and you giggled awkwardly, avoiding questions with vague responses and silly references to your muscular bodies. Prom came, and neither of you had dates. It seemed strange to me—two good-looking young men going to prom alone—but I dismissed it as jocks playing the field. Longing for details of the night, I came by, slightly after midnight, hoping to hear about the fun you two had had. That's when I saw you and Ricky strolling up the street. You didn't see me because you didn't know to look for me, but I saw you. And that's when you shattered my dream.

It happened so fast I almost convinced myself I'd imagined it. You two stood beneath the dogwood tree at the edge of the yard, almost hidden from view by low-hanging branches and full spring leaves. But I saw you. He took you by the shoulders and pulled you close, and you did not resist. I blinked several times, hoping the night had cast false shadows, but there was no mistake. His head bent slightly while yours lifted easily. When your mouths met, I covered mine. For whatever reason, I stared instead of turning away. Perhaps, again, I wanted to be sure of what I saw. Your arms embraced his waist, and I shivered with disgust. I tried to understand, but I didn't. How had you dated Marie all that time? And hadn't you let Vanessa taste you? Wasn't that enough to keep you straight?

I decided not to tell anyone. Even you. You might be shocked now, but don't be. It's of no consequence. That was a long time ago—back when I needed dreams to be happy.

I went on with life as we'd known it. I came by the next day and asked you about prom, and you told me all the lies you thought I wanted to hear. You named girls you danced with and boys who complimented your black-and-white tux. You admitted that someone had spiked the punch, which left you buzzed. I teased you about kissing girls, and you chuckled like a good son ought. It was all very real to me. Some days, I wished I hadn't seen what I had seen. Then, other days, I gave thanks, finally, for the indisputable truth.

You and Ricky hung out until he went to University of Nebraska on a football scholarship. I remember the day he left. You tried not to show it—the weight of love lost—but it hung heavy on you like a wet coat.

Your mother told you not to worry; friends always return. I said nothing. I hoped he was gone forever. But every other month or so, he came home and rekindled your joy. The moment you heard his voice, you bubbled over. I wonder if you remember him this way. Your mother said you two were best friends, nothing more. I nodded. She didn't know what I knew; she hadn't seen what I'd seen.

We dropped you at Lincoln University the following August. At forty, my role in your life diminished drastically. Actually, it pretty much ceased. I gave your mother money to pay your tuition and fees. I didn't ask about grades. I didn't come see you on weekends. I barely saw you on holidays. I didn't call. I thought of you all the time, but I made no effort to know you further. If you dated girls at Lincoln, I do not know. I never asked. I was afraid to know, really, scared that college might've freed you further. That's what people said education does—sets the captive free. I'm prone to believe that.

I do recall, though, your excitement after your first semester. Something had changed in you. You returned home confident and self-assured. You'd always known yourself—that was the basis of our tension—but now you seemed unapologetic about it. You weren't afraid of me anymore. You met me at the door and looked at me without blinking. "Hey, Dad. How you doin?" I didn't respond at first. I'd been used to your bowed head, your soft, murmuring voice. I think I was in shock. You continued staring until I answered, "I'm all right, I guess." We shook hands as I entered the house. We didn't hug—we never hugged—but I knew you were grown now. You smelled like a man. It's the stench of sweat and fresh ego. It's hard to describe, but I recognized it because Granddaddy told me the day he smelled it on me. He smiled a bit, proud, I think, that I wasn't weak and worthless, then warned playfully, "Watch yoself. A old man ain't nothin to play wit, boy. You think he ain't strong, but he'll fool ya." I didn't say this to you, but I thought it.

We sat in the living room, me, you, and your mother, as you told us about college life.

"I didn't care so much for my calculus class. The teacher was too strict. No partial credit at all! Either you got the problem right or the whole thing was wrong, so I wasn't really feeling him, but it was okay, I guess."

That meant you'd made an A.

"I loved my college comp class though." Your joy made us smile. "We read books I'd never heard of."

"Like what?" your mother asked.

"Like *The Mis-Education of the Negro* by Carter G. Woodson and *The Fire Next Time* by James Baldwin. That was my favorite!"

"What's it about?" she asked, and you answered with a lot of big words I didn't know. I nodded along anyway.

If I'd known who James Baldwin was, I might've understood the change in you.

"We protested, too," you said, proud of yourself. "Right on the quad in the middle of campus. News media came and everything."

"What did y'all protest?" I asked.

"South African apartheid."

You knew I didn't know what that was, so you spared my shame: "These white leaders of African countries, exploiting African people and taking the country's resources. Then they make the people live in squalor." You shook your head. "It's all the plan of international imperialism and European ethnocentrism." Again, I think you feared you had lost me, so you added, "People ought to govern themselves. White folks need to get the hell out of Africa. They've destroyed that whole continent."

I'd never heard you so political, so convicted about any social issue. You sounded like an activist from the '60s, and I wasn't sure I liked it. America tended to kill people like that. But you didn't need my permission, my approval for anything anymore. You had your own ideas, and all I could do was watch you change.

You spoke of frat parties and new friends from across America. You expected a 3.8, you said, sounding disappointed. Your mother laughed. I smiled. I didn't know what the number meant.

What I wanted to hear you never said. No mention of pretty girls or sneaking into the female dorm or wondering whether a young lady could come visit over the break. I almost asked directly if you had met anyone you really liked, but with your newfound confidence, I feared you might tell the truth, so I left it alone.

From one semester to the next, you came and went until graduating four years later. Your mother and I attended the ceremony. We were proud, sitting on the first row of bleachers like the lovely couple we once were. She took a thousand pictures of you with your friends, professors, the president. Then the three of us posed, smiling across our emotional divide.

Grandma would've been proud, I thought. She'd wanted a high school graduate in the family, and now there was a college grad, too. She'd heard—and believed—that education could provide a better life than the one she'd had, and she'd wanted someone in the family to experience it. From the looks of things, it would be you.

DECEMBER 23RD, 2003

After your graduation—May 1985—my world went silent. I smoked more often and socialized less. I stopped bathing every day, as I'd once done, and skipped the barbershop altogether. Coworkers noticed the change and asked if I was okay, and I said I was, but I wasn't.

Your mother told me, a few weeks later, that some big company in Chicago offered you a job and you took it. You didn't ask my advice. She said you'd be moving the following Saturday morning, so I came by to see you off.

"What kinda work is it?" I asked.

"Computer stuff."

"That's what you took up?"

"Yeah."

"Why didn't you study music or writing or something like that? That's what you're good at."

You frowned. "Not enough money in it."

I changed the subject.

"You got a place to stay?"

"Yessir."

"Plenty of money?"

"I don't know about *plenty*, but I guess I have enough."

I wanted you to ask me for some, to need me for something, but you didn't.

"You takin the Greyhound?"

"Yessir. I'll get a car after I work awhile."

I nodded and looked down. We were sitting, as usual, on the front steps. Your feet were as big as mine. You were a grown man.

I wanted to ask you to call me, but I couldn't. I don't know why. The words were right there, sitting on my tongue, begging for release, but I couldn't speak them.

"How long's the ride?"

"Bout twelve hours, I think."

"Mighty long time."

"Not too bad. Lots of time to read. And think about things."

Like what? I almost asked. For some reason, I saw Ricky Stanton in my mind. I wondered if he was in Chicago.

You turned and said suddenly, "Take care of Mom, Dad. Okay?"

"Okay. I will," I said, although you didn't seem to believe me. I wasn't sure exactly what you meant.

"She's not as strong as she appears."

Certainly I knew that, but you were implying something else, something I couldn't discern. I should've asked for clarity, but of course I didn't.

"I'll check in on her," I promised. It's the best I could think to say.

You nodded and slapped your thighs. "Well, I guess I'd better be going." You stood.

I was still sitting. "How you gettin to the bus station?"

"A friend of mine."

Who? Where'd you meet him? Is he going with you? Do you love him? "I can take you."

"Oh no, sir. He's already on the way."

You stepped toward the front door to go back inside. All the courage I could muster allowed me to say, "Take care of yourself, you hear?"

At first, you didn't respond. I wasn't sure you'd heard me. Then, when I looked up, you looked down with those big, beautiful, sad brown eyes and huffed, "I will, Dad."

I should've stood and hugged you. Should've insisted on taking you to the bus station. Or at least riding along with you and your friend. Should've put some extra money in your pocket. Should've asked for a contact number. Instead, I sulked and went home.

On the way, I pulled over for a smoke, and, leaning on my hood, I watched a woman and a little boy in the park throw a ball back and forth. He must've been six or seven, she in her midforties. A stray ball sent him dashing in my direction, and once he retrieved it, he looked at me and smiled.

"Hello, sir," he sang cheerfully. I loved his fearlessness.

"What's goin on, young fella?"

"Just playing catch with my mom. Wanna play?"

"Naw, I'm okay. Thanks anyway."

You'd think he'd have run back into his own world, but instead he asked, "You got any kids?"

His mother began walking toward us. "I have a son."

The boy's eyes dazzled. "How old is he?"

"Grown. Just graduated from college."

"What's his name?"

"Isaac."

"Mine's Isaiah."

"Nice to meet you, Isaiah. You're mighty friendly." I chuckled.

"My mom says I talk all the time."

She shook her head as she approached.

"Did you and Isaac play together when he was little?"

I hesitated, staring into his eyes. "Yes. Well, we tried."

"What do you mean?"

For some reason, I choked. "Isaac didn't like sports. Not really."

"I bet he liked playing with you!"

"Isaiah!" his mother scolded sweetly. "You don't know this man. Leave him alone."

"Aw, he's okay. Full of spunk, that's for sure!" I shook my head. "I like a boy like that."

"Always has been. Never meets a stranger, never stops talking."

"He has a son, too, Mom! Name's Isaac."

She embraced him from behind and clasped his mouth. There was no rebuke in her behavior. "You will have to forgive him." The boy's eyes beamed. His smile reminded me of you—once upon a time.

"How old's your boy?" she asked warmly. Her raspy voice, like a jazz singer's, rumbled in the wind.

"Twenty-two or twenty-three."

Isaiah frowned and wiggled free of his mother's hold. "You don't know how old your own son is?"

"Isaiah!"

"It's okay. Really it is." I laughed over my shame. She cackled along to help me.

"This son of mine! You don't ever know what he might say."

Suddenly, without warning, he sprang forward and hugged me. Too shocked to move, I stood still. Then, I bent slightly and returned the embrace. His mother shook her head but didn't object. It wasn't the embrace that weakened me; it was the strength of his hold, the way he squeezed for dear life. His mother smiled. When we released, the boy said, "Bring Isaac next time! We can all play together!"

"Hush, boy, and come on here!" she beckoned.

Before they turned to go, I asked, "Where's his father?"

She rolled her eyes and smirked. "At work. Where he always is."

They waltzed away, hand in hand. I stared after them. Tears came easily. *No, Isaac won't be coming with me*, I thought. I didn't even know where in Chicago you were going. In that moment, I realized I hardly knew you at all. If someone had asked me your favorite color, your best friend's name, your favorite book, your greatest fear, your shirt size—I wouldn't have known. I'd never inquired of such things, especially anything in your heart. The day you graduated from Lincoln, which certainly stands as the proudest day of my life, I thought to grab you and sing your praises. Yet the last time I'd touched you, really held you in my arms, you probably didn't remember. Neither did I.

DECEMBER 24TH, 2003

Charlie, my buddy at the post office, stopped me a month later and told me to go home. "Take some time and get yoself together, man, before they fire you." It wasn't nasty, his advice. In fact, he laid a soft, heavy hand upon my shoulder as he spoke. He said I stank and looked like shit. I followed his advice and clocked out.

Within minutes, I was home in the dark, smoking and staring at blank walls. I had no other friends to call. Bobby Joe and I had grown apart since he worked nights and I worked days, and I'd never built close relationships with other men. We didn't do that back in my day.

My first realization, during that dark time, was that I had rarely called you *son*. I always called you *boy*. When a father calls a boy *son*, he's declaring his pride in him. I didn't feel this way about you, even when you got grown. You had accomplished many things, but you still weren't the son I wanted.

I know this hurts, but I owe you honesty. It's the last debt I'll ever pay. Hopefully, it'll set you free. Most elders back home, Granddaddy included, were too proud to do this. He should've confessed many things, should've explained what I didn't know about him. I might've made different choices if he had. I'm trying to save you from that. If it hurts, these painful other pieces, just put them with what you know, and you'll see a whole, complete story. It'll all make sense in the end.

DECEMBER 25TH, 2003

Christmas day and I'm alone. No noise, no cheer, no family bustling about. My only company is the TV, which I don't watch most of the time.

I got up this morning and stared through the living room window, longing for a world I can't enter. People walk by sometimes, totally unaware that, just a few feet away, lies a desperate, dying man. I wonder if they'd come in if they knew.

DECEMBER 28TH, 2003

I was in my late forties now, spiraling out of control. Ironically, your mother saved me. She stopped by and frowned at the smell and squalor of my tiny living space and suggested that I treat myself better. I don't know why, but her compassion aroused life in me. She tried to smile but achieved only a kind smirk. Then, she touched me. Her soft, perfumed hand on my shoulder sent chills all over me. That touch had been my joy once.

She opened the curtains and said, "Come on, Jacob. This isn't you." I wanted to say *It is now*, but I didn't want to argue. Something about her voice, plus the penetrating light, birthed hope in me. It made me sit upright and behold, for the first time, the full magnitude of my dysfunction. "Get you a bath, honey," she said, "and stop laying around feeling sorry for yourself." I would've been offended except that she'd said *honey*. I'd always loved the way she said that.

Before departing, she said, "I brought you something," and extracted a book from her purse. She loved to read, as you know, and she said I needed to read this one, that it had been written *for men like me*. "I don't do no readin'," I said, which of course was true; still, she insisted I take it. "It'll teach you something," she said and laid it upon the arm of the sofa. I lifted it reluctantly and thanked her. "I might read it," I mumbled, "but I probably won't." She nodded and left it anyway.

It was *The Autobiography of Malcolm X*. My friend Charlie had mentioned it several times, but of course I hadn't read it. Now, with my own copy, I began reading because I was too miserable to do anything else. It rained hard the night I started, as if Heaven were trying to get my attention. I fumbled my way through the first few pages. It took me an hour to read that. So many words I didn't know, so many meanings beyond my reach. But I stayed with it. By midnight, I had pieced together the beginnings of little Malcolm's story. Here was a boy—a poor, light-skinned, naive black boy— who entered the world with nothing yet wanted everything. I'd never read a whole book before. I didn't even know books about black boys existed. Yet on every page I saw myself.

It would not be an exaggeration to say that, as I read, my imagination came alive. I began to conceive things I'd never thought of before. Like what it really meant to *be* black—not just *look* black. I discovered I hadn't loved being black; I had *accepted* it because I couldn't change it. I had not embraced it as a gift, had not seen it as divine. Neither had Malcolm at first. But as he read and studied black history, his self-love sprouted and became the basis of a new, affirming self. Now, I wanted to know what he knew.

I read for weeks. Often, I found myself mumbling out loud, trying to hold on to little threads of clarity within the story. What fascinated me most was that he changed his name. I didn't know a man could change his own name. When Malcolm became El-Hajj Malik El-Shabazz, I paused and looked outside as if suddenly in a new world. My whole consciousness was changing. My perception of reality was being disrupted. I was becoming a new man.

I soon returned to work and asked Charlie, "Do you think Malcolm really thought God was black?"

"Hell yeah!" he said. "He absolutely thought that. It makes sense, too, if you think about it. Everybody around the world thinks of God in their own image except black people. Indians have an Indian God, Asians have an Asian God. That makes sense, don't it?"

"Uh-huh."

"That's all Malcolm was saying."

The idea scared me, to be honest. But it excited me, too. Here I was, for the first time in my life, considering that God might look like me. *Me?* A poor black country fella who ain't never been much? I can't explain to you what this did to me. All I can say is that it changed me forever.

I almost called you the night I read about Malcolm and Elijah Muhammad parting ways. It crushed me to see a father and son treat each other like that. I think I simply wanted to hear your voice, to be connected to you. I listened to the dial tone for several seconds, but never dialed. What would I have said? You might've laughed at me for trying to read, after all these years, and the whole moment would've been ruined, so

I hung up. What I really wanted was for *you* to call *me*, but that didn't happen. You had no reason to. We weren't tied in any particular way, certainly not in our hearts. I stared at a blank ceiling, hoping, one day, to assure you I could never betray you the way Elijah Muhammad betrayed Malcolm, although you probably wouldn't have agreed.

The day I finished the book, I read the last sentence aloud then closed the cover slowly. It had opened my eyes as if, my entire life, I'd been asleep. I'd never known I could decide how to live, how to be in this world. Never knew I had the right. My people had submitted to life, and dealt with it the best they could. We didn't question God's ways. We simply accepted things and swallowed hard. No one asked, for instance, if I were happy as a child. It's not that they didn't care; it's that they didn't know they *could* care. We didn't think we were *supposed* to be happy. We were Negroes, after all, Colored people who were glad simply to be alive. Feelings were irrelevant. They had to be. There was no time in our stressful lives for emotions. Of course we laughed and cried and got angry like anyone else, but not for long. We were stoic and serious 90 percent of the time. Have you ever seen pictures of black people from the old days? They're never smiling. Life was too hard for that. We had to stay focused and live.

The only place to express emotion was the church, and even there, black men rarely did it. We kept our hearts to ourselves. I remember crying when I was about six years old because my puppy died. A man had offered him to me, and, to my surprise, Granddaddy said I could have him. I had to feed and water him and make a little doghouse for cold winter nights. Well, one night, it dropped below zero. Grandma told me to bring the dog inside, but Granddaddy insisted he'd be all right if I'd built the doghouse well. He'd told me to line it with hay and old rags, which I did, but by morning, my puppy lay stiff and frozen solid. I brought him inside and placed him next to the woodstove, hoping that a thawing might restore his life. It didn't. Granddaddy told me to dig a hole somewhere in the woods and bury him and stop all that crying. When I finished, he said, "Boys don't do that bullshit, son. Don't let me catch you doing it again." I said, "Yessir," and wiped my eyes. I'm not sure I ever loved that way again.

JANUARY 1ST, 2004

New Year's Day. Last night I heard folks shooting into the air. Parties and celebrations were all over the TV. I've always wanted to go to Times Square on New Year's Eve. Looks like a lotta fun. It's cold obviously—people shiver in coats, scarves, hats, and gloves—but no one cares. It's the energy, the excitement that's the point, and I wish I could sit right in the middle of it.

I wasn't sure I'd see another year, but here it is. I'll never make it to Times Square, but if you do, grab a whistle and blow it for me. That'll be the best this old man can do.

I think about grandkids all the time, but that's also a joy I'll never know. I'm sure you've not had any kids. Or been with a woman for that matter. But if you had, I would've loved them better than I loved you. They would've gotten the new me, the father you should've had, and you would've known how much I've changed.

★ ★ ★

Well, one book led to another. All the while you lived your life without me. You were grown, I believed, which meant you didn't need me. I'd gotten you to adulthood, so my job was complete. What a fool I was!

Each day, I discovered a new word or phrase until learning to read pretty good. I liked that I could read all by myself, without someone judging me. I also liked that reading took me places I could never go.

Charlie gave me a book called *Manchild in the Promised Land.* I'd never heard of it, but I started reading it one day on my lunch break. Like Malcolm, Sonny spent time in prison and struggled his way out of ignorance. Something about these kinds of stories intrigued me. I'd never been to prison and hoped never to go, but when brothers got locked up and used that time to strengthen their minds, I was proud. They were pimps and drug dealers, but they were also black men who didn't understand that the system was designed to destroy them. I hadn't understood this either. Yet living in Kansas City and watching black men work and still fail, I knew something was wrong.

All the books Charlie recommended were by and about black men except one—*The Color Purple.* It had stirred such controversy that he'd decided to check it out. "You might like it, you might not," he warned. I nodded, put the book in my locker at work, and left it for several days. Actually, I forgot about it. Then I saw a copy at your mother's house. (I'd stopped calling it *my* house by then.) She'd called and said you needed money, so I dropped it by. That's when I saw it on the coffee table in front of the TV. "I have that book," I said proudly. She froze. "You have *that* book?" Her emphasis offended me, but I let it go. "Have you read it?" I asked. She nodded, then added that the author had won several awards. "Please read it, Jacob. You really ought to read it."

Mister, one of the main characters from the book, reminded me of Granddaddy. He'd talked to Grandma as if she were a child, ordering her around the house and threatening her if she didn't obey. I was scared of Granddaddy, too, and rightly so. He meant what he said, and we all knew it. Fear found no place in him; instead, it lived in us whenever he arrived.

The Color Purple showed me that what we'd once called a man was actually a monster. Celie wrote letters to God about her abuser. Who could do a little girl that way? I sighed because I knew.

I could see Celie in my mind—dark, unattractive, short pigtails. I knew what men said to girls like her. I knew those men. I knew those girls. One, in our community, was named Hannah. She was slow, as people said back then, with one eye slightly off-center. Elders told us not to make fun of her, but we did. Her two-inch hair was always nappy and uncombed, and she wore what we called slave dresses. Her speech was never clear. She tried hard not to talk so kids wouldn't mock her, but sometimes she couldn't avoid it. We formed circles around her and teased her, touching her breasts and buttocks. No one, including her, would ever tell, so we didn't fear reprimand.

At fifteen, Hannah became pregnant. Everyone whispered about whose baby it might be. Boys teased each other about who had *fucked that ugly girl*. No one claimed responsibility.

Hannah started raising that child alone—she and her great-grandmother. The baby, a boy, was slow, too.

He died at age three. Before then, Hannah bustled about, feeding him and her great-grandmother as best she could. She washed clothes by hand, chopped wood, cooked, and cleaned house every single day. It wasn't much of a house, a shack, really, with a tiny living space, kitchen, washroom, and one bedroom where, in the winter, a bucket of water froze solid. But the house was immaculate. I know because Miss Eunice, her great-grandmother, beckoned me to their porch one summer day.

"Hey, boy! You!" she called faintly. I must've been thirteen or fourteen then.

"How you doin today, Miss Eunice?"

"Gettin by, I guess, for a old lady." She was funny without ever laughing. "Need you to help me out a minute."

"Yes, ma'am. What do you need?"

"Draw me some water from the well and sit it on the porch here. Go in the house and get that number three tub next to the stove. You can put the water in that. Old Arthur—" arthritis "—got me twisted up pretty bad, and that dumb girl o' mine done ate somethin she didn't have no business eatin. Sick as a dog."

I entered cautiously. We didn't generally go in other folks' houses back then, especially children, so I stepped with great care. Immediately I noticed how clean it was. Not a speck of dust anywhere. The sofa, old and covered with a floral sheet, sat with its back to the window, and a rocker with a homemade cushion rested across from it. Other items, a black woodstove, a tattered oval floor rug, and a small fragile-looking table on which a large, black Bible lay, seemed frozen in time. Careful not to touch anything, I eased around the rug and entered the kitchen, which was equally spotless. Grandma maintained our house well, but I'd never seen a place that tidy. I heard someone cough and shift behind a closed door, but I dared not open it. I almost called her name—*Hannah?*—but instead I minded my own business and did as I was told. I left the bucket on the front porch so Miss Eunice could have water throughout the day, and made my way home. Next morning, Hannah and Miss Eunice sat in church like nothing ever happened.

She didn't go to school—people said it would've been a waste of time—so she had no hope of a better life. Probably never thought about it. Or maybe she did. Who knows? I wonder sometimes what happened to her. I heard, many years back, that she moved away after Miss Eunice died, but to where? She didn't have any other folks.

With each page of *The Color Purple*, I thought of her. Every time Mister raped Celie, I wondered what Hannah must've thought as we groped and grabbed her. She cried sometimes, but made no sound. She never looked at us, but she knew who we were. Some days, I stood at the fence, staring as she lifted logs and bales of hay like a full-grown man. She tried to befriend me a time or two, but I rejected her. If the fellas had seen us talking, I would've been ridiculed. Their acceptance, back then, meant more than her kindness. If only I could apologize now, although I don't think God or Hannah would honor it.

One Sunday morning, as she walked before the church congregation, we began to giggle. Adults frowned and followed our eyes and found spots of burgundy blood on the back of her off-white dress. Miss Eunice, in her eighties then, hobbled on a cane and dragged Hannah through the side door of the church. We were instructed to mind our business, but we heard Miss Eunice tell Hannah, "You ain't got no sense, girl! Dumb as a rock! You don't know how a young lady takes care of herself? Huh? You too stupid to know when it's your time, chile?" The crisp slap across Hannah's face made us gasp. Miss Eunice sent her home to clean up and told her to be back before service ended. They lived at least two miles away. We watched Hannah dash down the dirt path and into the distance. We hoped she'd make it back in time. Yes, we mocked her, but we didn't want her to get a beating in front of everyone. Fortunately, she met the demand, though barely, and sat quietly in the rear of the church, panting and sweating profusely. Miss Eunice dared anyone to give her a napkin or towel. "Silly girl! She oughta know better!" her great-grandmother said. It was the only time we felt sorry for her.

I'd never thought of what it meant for a woman to live in perpetual fear of a man. And not just a woman, but a young girl like Celie who submitted because she knew she couldn't win. Grandma had been quiet and meek, for the most part, but she'd probably feared Granddaddy more than she'd feared God. I rarely heard her state an opinion or disagree with the old man.

I was happy Mister softened toward the end. Age granted him sight and revelation of his errors. His only vindication was to help Celie find her sister, and he did that, although he'd caused the breach in the first place. He was a broken, regretful, sad old man.

I went by the house to thank your mother for insisting I read the book, but when I arrived, guilt or shame or something robbed my voice. The door was open, so I let myself in and sat on the edge of the sofa, head bowed like a kid in trouble. At first, she didn't say anything, but then, sitting across from me in her reading chair, she asked, leaning forward, "You read the book, didn't you?"

I nodded.

She nodded.

We sat for a very long time, staring at everything but each other. I spoke first.

"I didn't know."

"Yes, you did. You didn't care."

I nodded again.

She blinked knowingly and said, "I'm proud of you, Jacob. Everybody gets to grow—even you."

Then she touched my hand. I looked into her eyes and said, "I'm sorry, Rachel."

"I know, I know," she repeated over and over.

"No, I'm not just sorry for myself. I'm sorry for us. For our family, for black people—"

"Yeah," she whispered. "Me, too."

I laid my other hand atop hers.

"What made you read it?"

I shrugged. "I don't know. Just been…in a place recently and thought it might help."

"Looks like it did."

JANUARY 4TH, 2004

I've spent the last few days staring at your fourth grade school picture. The one where you're wearing the red-and-green flannel shirt, and your hair looks like little mountain ranges of naps. You're smiling as if trying to show every tooth in your mouth. Your mother handed it to me one evening years ago and told me to put it in my wallet, so I did.

With each new wallet, I transferred it like a worn business card or an old receipt. I eventually forgot about it, to be honest, but day before yesterday I remembered it and pulled it out and stared at you as the sun went down.

Do you remember, years ago, when, on our way to Arkansas, you asked about my parents, my mother and father, but I didn't answer? I avoided that truth, but I'll tell you now. You have a right to know.

My grandparents had a daughter—my mother. I never

knew her because everything happened before my second birthday. She'd been a pretty girl, Grandma said, lean and shapely. But she wasn't acquiescent, which is to say she wasn't obedient. She would never live the life folks wanted for her. She had Granddaddy's stubborn spirit, so the two of them bumped heads from the start. He never mentioned her to Esau and me. Hearts were private back then.

But women were sometimes more open, so at sixteen I asked Grandma about my mother. She told me everything.

My mother had been a bold child. Belligerent. And Granddaddy hated it. The more he whipped her, the more unruly she became. She despised dresses and hair ribbons and Easter shoes. Grandma tried to protect her, but sometimes she couldn't. Bruises, scars, and bloody scratches from Granddaddy covered her arms and legs. The only time she was quiet was when Granddaddy knocked the voice out of her.

Eventually, she lost all desire to fight. She stopped challenging Granddaddy and became withdrawn.

At eighteen or nineteen, she married a boy from Plumerville, a little township ten miles away. They had a baby—your uncle Esau—a year later, then me eighteen months after that. Folks said my parents got into it about something one day, and my daddy shot my momma between the eyes.

Some said she talked back to him, which was certainly believable, others said she accused him of seeing another woman. Grandma didn't know exactly what happened. But after he shot her, he disappeared. They brought Momma's body and laid it on the cooling board behind the house. They also brought two babies and asked if Grandma and Granddaddy wanted us. If not, they'd give us to the state. My daddy's par-

ents were dead and none of his folks wanted two more mouths
to feed, according to Grandma, so she took us in. We were
boys, so Granddaddy complied.

According to Grandma, Granddaddy stood over my mother's
body for hours, but said nothing. She touched his arm, but he
pulled away. "Let me be, woman. I gotta do this my way." It
was the only time in fifty years he'd seemed moved by something, she recalled. I was barely walking.

Grandma's sorrow lingered in some unreachable place. "It's
like a stone," she said, "settled at the bottom of a stream. The
water's always moving, but the stone ain't."

I asked, "Did Granddaddy ever apologize to her? To you?"
Grandma chuckled. "For what? He didn't see nothin he
needed to 'pologize for. Told me weeks later she'd brought
it on herself. I asked if he was serious, and he said yes. 'Bible
tells a woman to submit,' he said. 'When we don't follow the
Word, this is what happens. You thought I was hard on her,
but I was trying to keep her alive. You shouldn't've contra-
dicted me the way you did. She was followin you.' I couldn't
believe he'd blamed me for her death. I didn't talk to him for
days. Then, one evening at the table, he said, 'You ain't got
to say nothin to me. The Bible speaks for itself. But we gon
raise these boys right. I'ma see to that.' And I guess we did.
Only other time he almost cried was the day your brother
died. He coulda died that day hisself."

Now you know the other person you sensed in the cemetery that day. It was my mother. I almost told you everything
right then, but I wasn't ready. You weren't either, I assumed.
But adults are always wrong about children's emotional capacity. Children don't carry the weight of history, so their

capacity for heavy things might be greater. But few adults believe this, so we pass along only what we think they can bear. Children wonder later why we didn't tell them everything so they could avoid our mistakes.

There were no pictures of my mother anywhere, which wasn't unusual for that time. There were no pictures of anyone in my grandparents' house. Actually, many black people avoided photographs in my day, afraid that their image might get in the wrong hands and be used against them. They said a picture contains your spirit, and I'm inclined to believe this, since cameras focus on and capture the eyes so well. Sometimes you can look at a person in a picture and when you move, their eyes follow you. I'm not sure what to make of this, but it's something spiritual, I believe. And back in the '40s, people protected their spirit with their lives. It's all they had.

After Grandma told me the story, I began dreaming about it. Rainy nights, for some reason, summoned the nightmare. I could hear the gun blast. She really was a pretty woman. Tall, like Granddaddy, but curvy and hippy like an August pear. She was dark like all of us, with big lips that might've appeared swollen. Her crowning feature was a long, slender neck that, like a stream, poured into her torso. Dangling earrings danced between her lobes and shoulders. She was elegant without effort. I saw her, in my dream, hanging clothes on a line when my father approached her. An argument developed, and he went inside and got a rifle. Trying to seem unmoved, she rolled her eyes and ignored him. That's probably what sparked his anger—that he produced no fear in her. He aimed and pulled the trigger without hesitation. The *boom* always awakened me. Some nights I lay still, staring into the dark, until the sun rose. Then I'd rise, shake off the terror, and go about my business.

I've spent a lifetime wondering if she would've loved me. But of course she would've. She was my mother.

I've told you about your uncle Esau, but I'm not sure I've been completely honest. I'm not sure I can. It's difficult to speak of a man this way, especially when he's your brother, but I'm gonna try.

Truth is, I worshipped him. Everywhere he went my eyes followed, wishing I were him. Boys weren't supposed to esteem other boys this way, but now I'm free to say that Esau was the most beautiful person I've ever known. Not the most beautiful *man*—the most gorgeous *human*. I've always believed this, but I couldn't say it. At times, I've thought I loved him. Really *loved* him. The way a man loves a woman. It's the only thing I know to compare it to. Esau mesmerized me in a way that's hard to explain. Sometimes I'd hide and stare at him until rebuking myself. Once, I watched him bathe in a tin tub in the kitchen. He stood in a bucket and soaped himself then rinsed with warm water from the stove. I peered at his naked form in awe. There were no blemishes, no excess fat, nothing misaligned, nothing disproportionate. Just a six-two perfect specimen of a man. Even his privates seemed measured to form. I can't imagine anyone more glorious.

I guess I'm saying I understand the love one man can have for another, although I don't mean it the way you do. But perhaps the difference isn't as great as I've thought.

JANUARY 17TH, 2004

I haven't written in a while. I couldn't. Too sick to eat or wash myself or do anything, I lay around for days, waiting. I thought my time had come. My only regret was that I hadn't finished with you. Then Charlie stopped by and refilled my prescription, so I got a little relief after a few days. He tried to get me to go to a hospital, but I wouldn't go. *I ain't dyin there*, I told him, and I mean that. I'm dying in my own house—where a man ought to die.

After *The Color Purple*, I became something of a reader. The more I read, the more I saw myself. Knowledge is a funny thing, Isaac. It informs by exposing. It shows you precisely how much you don't know.

In others' stories, I noticed how similar we all are. Everyone wants the same things. And everyone struggles with the same things.

Your mother phoned early one Sunday morning and told me that Alice Walker was scheduled to appear at Rainy Day Books down near 53rd and Shawnee Mission Parkway. You probably went there countless times, but I'd never been. I decided to go because I wanted to see this woman, face-to-face, who'd written a story so compelling I couldn't forget it.

I got there early, thinking it might be crowded, and I was right. People filled the store, chatting or browsing books, waiting for Ms. Walker to arrive. It was mostly women, and white women at that, which surprised me, but there were enough black women to make me stay. I didn't really want to talk, so I hid among a row of bookshelves and bided my time.

After a few minutes, I peeked and saw a group of white women cackling like spring hens. They were loud and un-ashamed, bearing matching T-shirts with writing I couldn't see until one stood and turned in my direction. The print read: *My daughter is a lesbian because she's supposed to be.* I read it over and over. The woman had no shame, no fear of others knowing. I wondered what her daughter thought, with a mother so embracing, so unapologetic about her child's being. And more, the woman seemed happy and proud. I didn't know what was written on others' shirts. I didn't look, and I didn't dare guess.

For the first time in my life, I felt wrong about my judgment of you. For so long, I never would've told anyone what you were, much less been proud about it. I'd hoped to hide you, to keep you concealed from the world. Lord knows I didn't think you were what you were *supposed* to be. Who'd ever heard of such a thing? God had *meant* for you to be that way? Maybe things were different for white folks. Perhaps they enjoyed the privilege to be whatever they wanted. But black folks had rules and restrictions we were supposed to abide by.

Still, after beholding that shirt, I felt ashamed. I envied this woman and her daughter, the way she bore and boasted her child's identity. There was something honorable about that, a sacred link between the two that felt so...*right*. Every child wants their parents' applause, and I had not applauded you. I'd celebrated your efforts, but not your being. Because I didn't agree. But the words on the shirt asked me, *Do you have to agree?*

Alice Walker was a soft-spoken, pretty black woman who spoke of the need for honesty in our stories. She said it saddened her that so many black men had found her work offensive when, really, she'd meant to heal us. The story was about Celie's strength, courage, and resilience. She'd accepted Shug's love, Ms. Walker emphasized, because no one else had found her worthy of it. Certainly no man. I shook my head.

JANUARY 18TH, 2004

When you were a kid, there was a man who lived around the corner from us on 54th and Indiana. People said he was *funny*. I saw him a few times, walking briskly to his mailbox and back as though afraid to be seen. Folks said he had no wife, no kids. Of course we knew what he was. No one bothered him though. We barely saw him. I never knew where he ate or shopped or went to church. His house must've been his entire universe. No light emitted from within the dark brown structure, day or night. I wondered where he'd come from, who his parents were. Or if he belonged to any people at all.

He died a few months after you went to college. The mailman suspected something because the mailbox was overrun, and neighbors complained of a terrible stench. Police and firemen carried the decomposing body out of the house and left the door wide-open.

I was stopping by our house one day when I saw it all. I

asked about the commotion and people told me the story. They said he lived alone with nothing. No TV, no furniture, no refrigerator. The house was practically bare. All the windows were covered with dark sheets, and for a bed he had an old army cot. A transistor radio sat on the floor next to it, along with a miniature lamp, which had no shade. He owned two pair of identical black pants, a few long-sleeved shirts, and several undergarments piled in a corner. Other than that, he had nothing.

I assumed he was gay, and that this was the result of that lifestyle. All they knew about the man was his name: Enoch Felder. It was on his mail. No one knew of any siblings or extended family to contact, but they did find a burial policy and a will tacked to the bedroom wall. It outlined what he wanted upon his death and how he wanted it done. He didn't want a funeral or even a viewing, but the funeral parlor held a short ceremony anyway in case someone knew him and perhaps loved him. One of the guys from the parlor said only one man showed up. He sat in the rear in all black with his head bowed the entire time. No one knew who he was. The funeral director played gospel music and read various scriptures, back and forth, for an hour, then asked the man if he wanted to say anything, but he never lifted his head. Just stood quietly and left. Can you imagine that? Only one person at your funeral? What kind of life is that?

I didn't want that for you. I wanted you to have your own family, your own joys, your own happy memories. I didn't believe two men could create that. They certainly couldn't have babies. And no one could've convinced me that a man's touch was as magical as a woman's. Men's hands, the men I knew, were rough and calloused. I wanted you to know a woman's tenderness.

The night I saw you and Ricky kissing under the tree, I was disgusted because you both seemed soft and fragile. You stared into each other's eyes with intense longing, and I wondered what had happened to you. I was so confused. I convinced myself this would pass. That it was a phase. But years went by and you never changed. I'm sure he didn't either.

I hope I'm not hurting your feelings. I'm trying to be honest here, to give you my heart, but it's difficult and messy, so you'll have to take it as it is—if you want it at all.

After you'd been in Chicago awhile, I tried to imagine your life there. I saw you, in my mind, marching the streets for gay rights, holding a sign that read We're People Too! or something like that. I prayed not to see you on TV. I would've been embarrassed about that.

Fear governed me back then. Men of my time were mean and hostile because we feared losing power. Feminists in the '80s declared that "manhood" was a socially conceived idea. It was an oppressive notion. In some ways, they were right. We had nothing if we didn't dominate others. We knew we could lose everything at any moment. Liberal women and gay men told us we were about to. Their freedom disturbed our self-worth—black and white men alike. That's why we lived in fear.

With or without us, women of all colors were marching to a new Zion. If we were going to be men, we'd have to do so on different terms. But we didn't know any other terms, so we sat and sulked in smoky bars and tension-filled households, waiting for women to break. Many fools are still waiting.

Our reaction to the gay rights movement was slightly different. Gay boys were first *boys*, which meant, in our eyes, manhood was their natural inheritance. We couldn't understand why they—why you—didn't want it. It was power and influence and godliness. Who wouldn't want that? We equated gayness with womanness back then. Even if they loved men, why did they act so feminine? Did they want to be women? Is that what gay meant? We had nothing but questions. And disdain. These were sons who would not embrace the benefits of manhood. You were one of them. You had no future, I believed, if you were *funny*. This rejection of manhood was the destruction of civilization. It was also the destruction of my personal existence because I had no power without it. If this sounds dramatic to you, you've misunderstood the gravity of our fears. How would the world survive if men loved only men? We took this seriously. We also took it personally. Women who loved women weren't as dangerous, we thought, for a good man could set her aright. We believed that men who loved men went against the fabric of society. They threatened to undo the natural order of things. This would be the end of the world, as we'd known it. What could be more frightening?

JANUARY 20TH, 2004

A few summers after you moved to Chicago, a young man came by the house looking for you. I'd stopped by after work, and that's when I saw him, from the rear, lingering on the front porch.

"May I help you?" I asked as I approached.

He said, "Um, yes. I'm looking for Isaac. Is this the right house?"

Dark purple boils covered his neck and arms. He was rail thin—almost skeletal—trembling, as if, any minute, he might fall over.

"Yes, it is. I'm his father."

He extended his right hand, and I took it, rubbing my thumb inadvertently across one of the sores. Quickly, I jerked away, scrubbing my palm against my pant leg. "Isaac's not here. He moved to Chicago."

Hope drained from his eyes. I thought he might cry.

He asked, "When did...he leave?"

"Few years ago."

Without transition, he nodded and lumbered slowly, carefully, down the front steps. Then he turned and asked, "Do you have...a phone number...for him?"

I went inside and wrote it on a corner of scrap paper and gave it to him. I was careful not to touch his hand again.

He thanked me and said, "Would you tell him...I came by? In case you...speak to him before I do?"

He said his name clearly, as if trying to assure I'd remember it, but I didn't.

"Where you from, young man?"

He coughed so violently I frowned. Then he extracted a used tissue from his pocket and scrubbed his mouth clean. "Just outside Columbia. Bout two hours...away."

"I see."

Almost to the street, he turned and mouthed, over his shoulder, *Thank you.* I shook my head and prayed never to see you like that.

Suddenly, I called, "How do you know Isaac?"

He swiveled slowly, completely. With head bowed and eyes closed, he released an audible sigh. Seconds passed before he looked up and into my eyes.

"We were friends. Once."

He got into the passenger side of a car and someone drove him away. I went straight to the kitchen sink and scrubbed my hands raw. The whole encounter was dreadful. His face, all sunken and bony, had no fat at all. Every step seemed to exhaust him.

I've wondered, all these years, if he'd been your lover. My

prayer is that you're healthy and that you've steered clear of that devastating thing. I certainly hope so. If you haven't, stay under a doctor's care. I can't imagine that that young man saw a doctor regularly. He bore the look of death. If he's still living, he is most blessed. If he's dead, as I suspect he is, and if you loved him, I am sorry for your loss. And I'm sorry most that I can't remember his name.

They made a huge quilt in Washington, DC, in 1986 or '87 to commemorate the lives of those lost to AIDS. Seeing that boy made me think of it. It was large enough to cover the entire White House lawn. I saw it all on the news. Parents and loved ones came. I felt sorry for them, the parents. From the looks of things, there were more whites than blacks, which made me believe the disease was theirs. Our boys had gotten it from them.

I started dreaming up the lie I'd tell if anyone asked me about you. I had rehearsed the whole thing in my mind. Her name was Victoria, who we called Vickie, and she was tall with long straight black hair, a coke-bottle shape, and golden-brown skin like your mother's. Her long, shapely legs reminded folks of Tina Turner. You met her in college and had been dating since. I would tell people, although I didn't know a date, that a wedding was certainly on the way. Her parents, members of New Hope Baptist Church, were good, upstanding folks who believed in education and family values. They lived in Raytown. Vickie had an older brother studying medicine at Meharry, down in Nashville. You two wanted a large family, and a ranch-style home in the suburbs. And on and on. I'd thought the lie all the way out, down to her parents being from Vicksburg, Mississippi. Why Vicksburg I don't know, but that's what I would've said.

People never asked. I believe now that they knew the truth. Guys at work spoke of their own boys with joy and pride, but never mentioned you. They knew your name. I had spoken of you a few times as a child—a brilliant, creative child—but in your teenage years, I didn't say much. They sensed something wrong. I could tell. When speaking of their sons, they'd steal glances at me, as if sympathizing for my loss.

Still, I was prepared. I stayed prepared for years. And with each year, the story became fuller, more developed, as if I were writing a full-blown novel. You and Vickie married in her family's front yard in Raytown. Your mother and I sat together. There was live music and catered food and dancing into the night. The boys from work stood around in church suits, talking shit and drinking far too much. The most memorable part was you and Vickie running to the awaiting car as we showered you with rice. The boys patted my back and teased about you being far more handsome than I ever was.

A year later, you and Vickie presented my first grandson. His name was Esau. I held him close. He grew into a fine little boy, lean and strong. Baseball was his passion. I went to his games. We were close. Of course we were. I was his grandfather.

JANUARY 23RD, 2004

There is one other thing I must mention, one sorrow neither of us can ignore. It changed my life forever, as I'm sure it did yours, yet there were pieces of this sorrow, even moments of beauty, that you couldn't have known. Perhaps knowing it now will comfort you.

She'd told me she wasn't feeling well, and I could see it in her eyes—the jaundiced look of death. I'd stopped by the house to make sure neither of you needed anything. I told her something was wrong; she didn't look like herself. She nodded slowly and said she had a cold that wouldn't break. It was more than that. I knew. I think she knew, too. I returned a few days later and saw the same gray, gloomy mist covering her eyes, but her spirit was better, so I relaxed. I didn't want to know. She denied it, too, as long as she could.

Months later, she called and asked me to drop by. When

I did, she told me to come in and have a seat. That's when I knew for sure.

She touched my knee, like old friends might do. She cried awhile before speaking. We held hands as she purged everything she'd been carrying. She said, finally, "Breast cancer." Just like that. I couldn't face her. I chewed my bottom lip as she continued: "Could be six months, could be a year. No longer. Please," she said, her hands trembling, "find Isaac. I know you two don't see eye to eye, but you're all you've got now. Both of you." She'd written your address and number on the back of a take-out flyer, although I already had your number. "He thinks you don't like him. I know that's not true, but he needs to hear it from you." I promised I'd call. And I did.

"Hello?" you said.

"Hey, boy. How's it going?"

"Fine. Is this Dad?"

"Yeah. Thought I'd…check on you."

You didn't believe that, so you said simply, "Yeah. Okay."

"How you doin?"

"Fine."

"How's the weather?"

"Cold."

"You need anything?"

That's when you paused and asked, "Is something wrong, Dad?"

"Oh no! I just…um…wanted to make sure you was okay. Hadn't heard from you in a while. Thought I'd call."

"You seen Mom lately?"

"Yeah, I was over there yesterday."

"How's she doin?"

"Um...she's...fine. Just fine."

For several seconds, we held the phone in silence. I saw, in my mind, your scowled expression, wondering why I had called *for real*.

"You like your job?"

"It's okay. Pays the bills."

For the life of me, I couldn't think of anything meaningful to say.

"Dad, you sure everything's okay?"

"Oh yes. Everything's...good." I swallowed hard, then added, "Take care of yourself."

You said, "Okay," and hung up.

I was so disappointed. I almost called you back, but instead I held the receiver as regret gathered in my heart. I couldn't say what was wrong because I promised your mother I wouldn't. I tried to sound lighthearted and cheerful, but I failed. I never did say *I love you*. That's the reason I'd called. That's what I'd promised your mother I'd say.

You didn't learn of her illness until Thanksgiving. You drove home, and when you arrived, I met you at the edge of the street. I smiled and embraced you, and you frowned. You knew something was up.

When you saw her standing in the living room, half her size, you froze and stared. She mumbled, "Hi, baby," and you crumbled to the floor. Too thin and weak to disguise it, she knelt beside you and rubbed your head as you wailed. Disease had darkened the light in her eyes and eaten most of the flesh from her bones. Her face looked sunken and sad. I cried, too, watching you accept the inevitable. "It's cancer," she said. "Breast cancer." You laid your head in your mother's lap while she closed her eyes and assured you you'd be okay. I should've joined you, at your mother's feet, weeping for all she'd been to you. To us. Instead, I sat on the sofa and waited.

Hours passed, it seemed, before you rose. "Why didn't you tell me?" you asked her, but she smiled and explained that she didn't want to worry you. She added that she'd sworn me to silence, so she asked you not to be angry with me. You shook your head and cried all over again. She didn't tell you she had six months to live. She simply said, "It won't be long, baby." You asked, "How long?" and she said she didn't know. I turned away. I thought you should know, but she'd begged me to honor her wishes, so I did.

You told her you were moving home, but she insisted you stay in Chicago. It would be worse seeing you every day, she said, knowing the pain you were going through. "I couldn't handle that," she whispered. "I want you to live your life, son. Thrive. Go after your dreams. That'll make me happy." Your head kept shaking with disbelief. Our eyes met, finally, yours and mine, and you knew why I had called.

All three of us brooded in silence as the sun went down. You and your mother shifted to the sofa, so I took the armchair. Your head rested on her shoulder and she cupped your face with her palm. I stared through the window, wondering if my mother and I would've been so close.

Wrapped in each other's embrace, you found solace in some private, internal place. Your free, open touch unsettled me. No one had ever touched me that way. And I'd avoided touching others. Even when you were a kid, I didn't hold you much.

I held you as a baby, but once you started talking, I stopped touching you. Nurturing felt awkward to me. Now, it's all I long for.

Your mother died on Monday morning, February 7, 1994, three months after that Thanksgiving. I was fifty-three, you were thirty or thirty-one. Her doctor called me at work, and I knew she was gone. She'd been in and out of the hospital for weeks, choosing, in her last days, to die at home. Like I'm doing now.

Yet one hospital visit remains fresh in my memory. It was a Friday night, as I recall. I'd just gotten paid, so I bought a bouquet of flowers. Assuming your mother was asleep, I set them quietly upon her nightstand and eased into the chair next to her bed. She smiled suddenly, peeking from one eye, and said, "Green carnations. You remembered. Thank you."

I smiled, too. "You're welcome."

She turned her head slightly, opened one eye to view them, and nodded. "You remembered. How thoughtful. They're beautiful."

"I'm glad you like them."

She swayed slightly, as if a song played in her head. I reached to touch her hand and she did not pull away.

"I'm tired of being sick and sad," she slurred. "I'm gonna die. That's all. I don't wanna be sad about it anymore."

What do you say to that?

She sighed heavily. "Tell me something funny, Jacob. Make me laugh for a change. I'm tired of crying."

So I stood at the foot of her bed and said, "There was a woman back home named Miss Hallelujah."

With eyes still closed, she smiled and whispered, "You always was a fool, Jacob Swinton!"

"Seriously! That was her name!"

"That was *not* her name."

"Well, that's what we called her."

Your mother's head shook slightly, and I continued: "Anytime someone said good morning or good evening or whatever, she replied, 'Hallelujah! Oh, praise His name!'" I mimicked her voice, and your mother chuckled, and then frowned as if it hurt. "She was single, she said, because no man could ever love her the way Jesus could. We thought she was crazy, walking around in long skirts and high-neck blouses, but elders told us to let her be. If she was gon be crazy about anything, Jesus was a good choice.

"Well, me and Granddaddy saw her in town one Saturday afternoon, and when he spoke, she lifted her hands and said, 'Hallelujah, Mr. Abraham! Oh, praise His name! God is a good God! Yes, He is!' Granddaddy nodded and said, 'Every day. Don't know what I'd do without Him.' Her hands flew up. 'Can't nobody do you like Jesus! When you're lonely, He'll comfort you! When you're sick, He'll make you well again! I'm gon praise Him every day I live! Ain't no rock gon cry out for me!' Granddaddy took a risk and asked, 'You don't want no man, Hallelujah? No kids? Family of your own?' I guessed she was probably in her early forties. Anyway, she threw her nose in the air and said, 'I don't need no man, Mr. Abraham Swinton!' She stomped angrily. 'Long as I got King Jesus, I don't need nobody else!' Suddenly she started singing, 'I woke up this morning with my mind, stayed on Jesus!

Hallelu, Hallelu, Hallelu—jah! It ain't no harm to keep yo mind, stayed on Jesus!' and walked off, speaking in tongues.

"Granddaddy shook his head as I chuckled along. Well, months later we saw Miss Hallelujah again, this time obviously pregnant. She lifted her head high—" I exaggerated the gesture "—and said, more boldly than before, 'Hallelujah! He's worthy to be praised!' Granddaddy's eyes bulged and he said, 'He sho must be! Looks like He comforted you all night long!'"

Your mother rolled to her side, jerking and laughing. I hadn't thought about Miss Hallelujah in years. Seeing Rachel happy made me happy, and, for the moment, we defeated old woman Death.

"You know you lyin, Jacob Swinton," she whispered after regaining composure.

"No I'm not! That's a true story! I was standing right there when he said it. I almost got in trouble, I laughed so hard."

She panted heavily, like a tired race dog. A nurse entered and asked what was so funny, but we couldn't explain it. She told me to be careful, your mother needed rest and quiet, but when the nurse left, Rachel said, "Tell me another one."

"I don't just make up stories, woman!" I teased.

"Yes you do," she murmured. "You been lyin your whole life!"

I could've been offended, but decided not to be. What did it matter now anyway?

"You remember a man I used to talk about named Mr. Elihue?"

She shook her head.

"Yes, you do! The one who was always testifyin in church. You remember me talkin bout him, don't you?"

"Uh-uh."

"Okay, well, he was a little man, bout five-five, with the loudest voice you've ever heard. Everything he said, he screamed. If you spoke to him quietly, he'd shout, 'Hey! How you doin?' as if you were miles away."

Your mother snickered at my antics once again, and I just knew the nurse was coming to put me out, but she never did.

"One Sunday morning, Mr. Elihue stumbled into church, drunk as a skunk. We knew he drank sometimes, but usually not on Saturday nights because he loved to testify Sunday mornings. His wife, Miss Myrtle, grabbed his arm, trying her best to get him to go home, but he pushed her away and sat where he always did—on the end of the first pew. We kids snickered softly, waiting to see what the deacons might do, but they didn't do anything. So Mr. Elihue, loud and off-key, sang the opening hymn right along with the rest of us: 'Je-sus keep me near the cross! There's a precious fountain.' Women frowned and shook their heads. One said, 'Lord have mercy! Somebody oughta do somethin bout that man!' But no one moved. He clapped and sang so loudly deacons stared and narrowed their eyes, but they didn't remove him."

Your mother smiled again. This time she opened her eyes a bit.

"As always, Pastor asked if anyone wanted to testify, and, to no one's surprise, Mr. Elihue jumped up like he'd been stung by bees and slurred, 'Yes! Yes, I do! I can tell you bout the goodness of de Lawd!'"

I stumbled around, mocking the man, while your mother,

holding her side, declared softly, "You oughta be shame o' yourself!"

"This is a true story, Rachel! I ain't makin nothin up! He fumbled like he might fall over, talkin bout how good God is. The more he talked, the more excited he became, until he screamed, 'I'm blessed throughout the day, I'm blessed throughout the night! All my *chil'ren* blessed! My *wife* blessed! My *cows* blessed! My *crops* blessed! My *well water* blessed!'"

By this point, your mother's arms hung limp over the sides of the bed. Tears streamed her eyes, but she didn't bother wiping them.

"'My *barn* blessed! My *mules* blessed! My *fruit trees* blessed! My *pond* blessed! My *house* blessed! My *food* blessed! Shit, everything I got is muthafuckin blessed!'"

I barely said the last line before crumbling to my knees. I hadn't laughed that hard in years. Your mother, moaning and shivering with glee, rolled from side to side, panting, "Shut up, Jacob Swinton! Just shut up! Don't say another word to me!" I reached for the bed frame, trying to steady myself, but it was no use. Every time I heard Mr. Elihue in my mind, screaming loudly before the congregation, I became weaker and weaker. Several minutes passed as your mother twisted and squirmed, trying with feeble might to find her breath again. Together, we screeched until eventually both of us collapsed—she in the bed, me in the chair—laughing continuously as the sun went down. I touched her hand again and she squeezed mine, and we dosed off without saying another word. Somewhere in the middle of the night, I could've sworn I heard Death cackling still.

JANUARY 24TH, 2004

She went home the next day, declaring she'd never return to the hospital, and she never did. A month later, she was gone. When I arrived home that day, Angie, her girlfriend from the shelter, met me on the front step. We hugged and blinked tears. Your mother went peacefully, I think, coiled in a fetal position. Your college graduation picture stood on her nightstand. You looked so much like her that beautiful spring day. The smile, full lips, thin nose. All she ever wanted was to go to school, and you were the closest she got.

I remember calling you again. You answered and heard my voice, so you knew. I said, *Hey, son,* and you said, *When did it happen?* and I said, *We found her this morning,* and you said *Where?* and I said, *In bed,* and you said, *Good. She went easy.* We were silent awhile, breathing hurt and loss, then you said, *I'll be there tomorrow. Wait for me.* Then you hung up. I didn't know what *wait for me* meant, but I assumed you wanted to be part of the planning process, so I waited until you came. She wasn't my wife anymore, but she was still your mother, so I deferred to you.

When you arrived, we hugged—the second or third time in our lives—like business partners closing a deal. I admonished, "You gotta be strong, Isaac," so you composed yourself quickly, and said, "We'll go to the funeral home tomorrow and make arrangements." I nodded, and that was that.

But that night, I heard you. You probably thought I was asleep, but I wasn't. The house was dark except for a small stream of light coming from your mother's bedroom. I heard mumbling, so I rose from the sofa and followed the sound. That's when I saw you, through a crack in the bedroom door, sitting on her bed, talking to her as if she was right there beside you. You weren't sad at all. Not anymore. You were gesturing and smiling and frowning as if you two were having a whole conversation.

"I'm fine, Momma. Don't worry."

You paused.

"Yes, Momma, I love someone. I do."

You paused again.

"I don't know who he looks like! But he's beautiful."

You beamed with joy for a moment.

"No, I'm not gonna tell Dad. Why would I do that?"

I frowned.

"I have my own life to live, Mom. Dad has his."

Pause.

"He doesn't wanna know. He's never asked me before."

Pause.

"I won't do that to myself. I won't."

Your head shook violently.

"I'm thinking about buying a house."

Pause.

"I like Chicago. It's cold, but it's nice."

This time you paused a long time, and when you spoke again, your eyes brimmed with tears.

"Is it pretty over there, Momma?"

You smiled.

"Will you send me a sign that you're okay?"

She must've said something funny, for you laughed so loudly you covered your mouth and rolled on the bed. That's when I walked back to the sofa and returned, in my mind, to Arkansas, all those years before at the cemetery, and finally I understood that you had a gift, a special relationship with the Invisible, that I knew nothing about.

I cried that night. I missed your mother for sure, but it was your words that devastated me. You wanted nothing to do with me. You thought I wanted nothing to do with you. You had no intention of sharing your life with me, and that hurt more than your mother's death. That's right. I watched her die; I knew it was coming. But I'd hoped that you and I, after burying Rachel, might find common ground and build some sort of life that included both of us. Now I knew that wasn't going to happen.

The next day, we picked out a beautiful white casket with gold trim. Well, you picked it out and I went along. You chose from her closet a yellow dress, which you said she loved, so that's what we buried her in. She loved yellow roses, too, so you had one placed in her folded hands.

Those days between her death and the funeral were the

only days we'd spent alone since our trip to Arkansas. I stayed
at the house with you in case you needed anything, but you
didn't. We moped for three days, eating, as we did so many
years ago, at the little oval table in the kitchen, but saying
very little. I cooked and washed dishes; you sorted through
your mother's papers and personal things, deciding what to
keep, what to throw away. You asked if I wanted anything,
and I said only our wedding picture. It lay at the bottom of
a trunk, enclosed in a cheap golden frame. Your mother and
I looked like kids, you said. We *were* kids, I said. You took
the photo albums, which marked your growth from infancy
to adulthood, and you also took her books. Later you found,
wrapped in a pretty lace handkerchief, your mother's wedding ring. You asked if I wanted it, since I'd bought it, but I
said no. You then asked if you could have it, and I nodded. I
wondered what you'd do with it. It later occurred to me that
you might give it to a man. I hoped you wouldn't. It wasn't
meant for that.

Clothes, shoes, and accessories went to the Salvation Army.
When you finished, the house was bare. Only furniture remained. It was yours, I told you, the house, since your mother
was gone. I'd paid it off recently, and this was part of your
inheritance. You looked around and said softly, "I don't want
it. I'll never live here again." Too hurt to respond, I simply
nodded. *I've worked a lifetime to own this house, and you don't
even want it? Fine! I'll keep it for myself.* No need paying rent
elsewhere, I decided, when I own an empty house.

JANUARY 26TH, 2004

I realized how much I loved your mother the day we buried her. She'd outgrown me over the years, but still I loved her. I thought at times that I despised her, but I didn't. No other woman had ever occupied my heart. The night we spent together in the hospital, my original adoration resurfaced. I wanted to take her in my arms and kiss her and ask her to trust me again. *I've been a fool*, I might've said. *No one else has ever made me happy.*

At the funeral, Death teased me. I didn't see her, but I sensed her. Small whiffs of air, like breath, grazed my neck, and each time I rubbed it, I heard faint laughter. Later, she told me it was her. We've become friends over the years. She saw my day coming, she said, and wanted to get acquainted before I'd have to trust her. We speak quite often now. She said she never understood why her presence saddens others. She is the bearer of joy and life's perfect fulfillment. All she ever does is accompany people into eternity. Everyone dreams of it—and fears it—but it is a beautiful existence, she said. A paradise. No one who's gone has ever wanted to return.

I didn't know this then. All I knew, all I felt, was loneliness. The perfect life I'd dreamed with your mother never came to pass. Our living room became my personal tomb: dark, quiet, lifeless. Everything I'd loved I'd destroyed. You don't know—I hope you don't know—the feeling of losing everyone you ever loved. You're left with only your own hurt and regret. All you do is relive mistakes and wish you could undo them. You never can.

You left hours after the funeral, headed back to Chicago. I was ashamed of what little I knew about you. You lived in a world I had never entered. But you were my son. My *only* son. Still, that didn't make me come see you. Once your car vanished, I returned to the house, consumed in a frightening silence. For days, the world stood still. I didn't speak, watch TV, or listen to the radio. I'd been given a week off work, so there were no necessary human encounters. Only Silence and me. Silence isn't always quiet though. It troubles a man's soul, forcing him to admit what he'd rather forget.

So when Death came to me after your mother died, I wasn't surprised. She materialized one evening, smiling sweetly, draped in layers of flowing blue. I considered the figure might be your mother's spirit, but Death identified herself and assured me she wasn't there for me. She was there to collect the last of your mother's memories. When people die, she said, they want to leave unpleasant memories behind. Such remembrances are heavy and irrelevant in the afterlife, people think.

Plus, they make travel through the universe difficult. But this is not allowed. Everything the heart has ever known must accompany it into eternity. Regardless of the pain. Only then can a person see God. A whole heart is Heaven's requirement.

I had so many questions, but Death wouldn't answer them. I would have to go with her, she said, if I were to learn her secrets, so I stopped asking. Last year, I asked if I could write you before I go. She happily obliged. There was no rush, she said. It's fear that people battle most, she told me, but once they surrender, they take her hand and go willingly. We talk all the time now. She says I can come whenever I'm ready, and I'll be ready soon—after I settle up with you.

JANUARY 27TH, 2004

I moved back into the house a few weeks after the funeral. I was fifty and back where I'd started from. The house felt empty and unwelcoming. It seemed smaller somehow, too. I slept on the sofa. Your mother's room held too many memories, and your room too much pain. Standing in your doorway, I felt anxiety, hurt, and longing. I closed the door softly and never reentered.

Many evenings after work, I tried to read but couldn't concentrate. I reread sentences twenty times until I simply gave up. Still, I needed something. Silence and loneliness were driving me mad. I tried hanging out with the boys a few times, but we had nothing in common anymore. They spoke of lives and problems I only wished I had: nagging wives, disobedient grandchildren, money-hungry sons. With each encounter I sank deeper into an abyss, so I stopped going.

Sometimes I walked the neighborhood at night, trying to get my spirit back, but I just couldn't find it.

One night, while walking down Paseo, I approached a little church near the corner of 63rd Street. It couldn't have been much larger than our living room, but the congregation was boisterous with tambourines and drums. I think it was a Pentecostal church, but I never bothered knowing. The front doors swung wide, inviting strangers inside. I never even meant to stop, but as I got closer, I heard the choir singing a song that simply said "God has smiled on me," and I couldn't move. I had never heard the song before, but its lyrics pried straight through my pain. I began to cry. The more they sang, the more I wept, until tears dampened the front of my shirt. Every disappointment, frustration, and loss resurfaced until I mourned like Jesus must've at Lazarus's tomb. It's the only time the Bible says he wept, a preacher once said, so he must've *really* wept. I'd thought I'd outgrown God, but it was just the church I'd had enough of. Although here I was, trembling at the entrance, being healed by the very thing I'd thought I didn't need anymore.

Suddenly someone touched me. I looked up and saw a tattered, unkempt homeless man staring back at me. He smelled of urine and body odor, but his eyes, like mine, were moist. He planted himself next to me on the steps.

He said, "Every man needs a li'l mercy every now and then. Know what I mean?"

I nodded. I'd expected him to be crazy or at least nonsensical, but his was the sanest voice I'd heard in a while.

The choir sang another song, something about joy in the midst of sorrow, while the stranger and I sat together, thinking our own independent thoughts. When they finished, I asked, "What's your name, man?"

He laughed as if I'd made a joke. "Been a long time since anybody asked me that."

"What do you mean?"

"I mean, nobody asks me my name. They stare at me or pity me with change or a dollar or sometimes food they don't want. But they never ask my name."

I nodded slowly, remembering times I'd done exactly that. "People don't mean no harm," I offered defensively. "They just don't care enough."

"You're right about that. That's probably why I'm here."

I turned to face him, prepared to hear his story, but he stood abruptly and said, "Take care o' *yourself*, my brother. Ain't nobody else gon do it but you," and began walking away.

"Thanks, man," I said, unsure he had heard me.

"Thank *you*," he tossed over his shoulder. Then, after a few more steps, he paused and turned. "Zacchaeus. That's my name. My momma hoped it would make me wealthy. Guess the joke's on her." He walked a bit farther, then, once again, shouted over his shoulder, "Or maybe on me!"

Once he left, I prayed out loud for the first time in a very long time: "Father God, help me. I don't know what to do." I didn't bow my head. "Grandma use to say when you don't know what to do, go to God in prayer. Well, here I am." A cool breeze grazed my face, and I smiled: "I know I failed, Lord. I know that. But I wanna fix things if I can. If You'll help me. Just tell me what to do, and I'll do it." I paused, staring into the bright, nighttime sky. "Do me like you did Daniel in the lion's den, and I'll forever give your name the glory, the honor, and the praise." That's how they had taught us to pray back home, so that's what I said.

For a while, I lingered, watching cars go by. Then, once again, I looked up at the star-spangled sky. I'd surveyed it some nights back home, but I'd never really noticed how the heavens move. Stars shoot across the cosmos then fade to nothing while the moon creeps around, hiding behind shifting clouds. It was remarkable to see.

I prayed some more: "Forgive me, God, for the way I've treated my son. I don't know where he is or what he's doing, but keep him safe, keep him in your care. He's all I got." In my mind, I saw your mother, smiling. "Bring him back to me. I don't always understand him, but teach me, Father God, how to love him."

Years later, I realized I had prayed the wrong prayer. I should've asked God to send me to you, but I didn't. So I spent years waiting for you—while you've spent a lifetime waiting for me.

That song, "God Has Smiled on Me," had been written by a man named James Cleveland. I went to the music store and bought several of his albums. He has a thick, coarse baritone that reverberates like a storm. It became a ritual for me, listening to James Cleveland in the evenings as I prepared dinner or sat on the sofa. His voice reminded me of home: the land, the people, the will to survive.

I'd never really thought of it before, but listening to Cleveland, I noticed how much, and how often, black people sing of water, ships, and troubled seas. I knew something about trouble, and I liked the notion of a ship standing ready to deliver me. We'd come to America on ships—very large ships—that surely had been accompanied, at times, by turbulent water. James Cleveland and the Angelic Choir sang a song that spoke of a ship being tossed to and fro by an angry sea until Jesus says, "Peace be still," and the waters calm. It's a fascinating story and a soothing melody I never tire of hearing.

One night, I closed my eyes, right there in the living room, and swayed as the song played on the stereo. It wasn't Heaven I envisioned though. It was Arkansas. Granddaddy, Grandma, Esau, the land. Maybe that was Heaven to me.

So I did a mighty spontaneous thing: I got up, grabbed my keys and a jacket, and drove home.

JANUARY 28TH, 2004

I traveled through the night and entered Alma, Arkansas, just ninety minutes from home, as the sun rose. A short gas stop, a sausage-egg breakfast sandwich, and I was on I-40 east, headed to Blackwell. The weather was cool but not cold, so I lowered my window and inhaled the scent of home. It's the smell of honeysuckle and freshly smoked pork. I always loved hog killing time of the year. Nothing beats the aroma of fried pork chops or baked ham.

My other favorite time of year was spring, when jonquils and wild roses burst free across the land. Your uncle Esau and I used to pinch the end of the honeysuckle bloom and extract the inner tube, which is coated with nectar so sweet it tastes like honey. I suppose that's why it's called honeysuckle. Only when I left Blackwell did I realize how much I missed the aroma.

But now, with cool, crisp country air grazing my face, I smelled it once again and knew I was almost home.

When I arrived, I silenced the engine and sat still. Birds chirped in the distance, wind danced across fields, squirrels played chase between treetops. The whole scene welcomed me. The old house had practically collapsed, but that was no surprise. Without upkeep, it was doomed to fall one day. So many memories in that shack—some good, some worth forgetting. But I was home, and, for some reason, I felt the need to be there. Perhaps I'd gotten old and sentimental, for even the grass seemed greener, trees taller, fields more golden than I remembered. Then I smiled: this was the scene you had painted all those years before.

Suddenly, I heard an engine approaching. From down the road came a red beat-up '76 Datsun pickup fumbling toward me. I didn't know who it was, but the driver weaved as if drunk or in a hurry.

I saw a raised left hand before I recognized Mr. John Davies. He pulled the little battered truck onto the side of the road and rolled out. "Whatchasay there, young fella!" he shouted so loudly I almost laughed. Mr. Davies had once been Granddaddy's friend. He was always loud and fat, but now he was louder and fatter.

"I'm doin fine, Mr. John. How you doin, sir?"

"Fair to middlin, for a old man. Arthritis got me pretty bad, but, hell, somethin gon getcha sooner or later." He chuckled and hobbled, as he always had, closer to where I stood. Most of his teeth were gone and the wrinkles in his face had deepened into crevices. They looked like intersecting valleys of black flesh, the crisscrossing craters, and I wondered just how old he was. He was old when I was a kid. His distinctive sway had deteriorated into a cane-assisted limp. I'd assumed he'd passed on, but there he was.

He stared and looked around. "My daddy used to say, 'Time waits for no man.' And, boy, if that ain't the truth!" He cackled. "Gon pass if you do somethin, gon pass if you don't."

I nodded.

"This what I do every day. Git up and drive around and see what the Good Lawd done done. Anything change I can tell you. I notice things. It's what old men do." He cackled again. "What chu doin here?"

"Just got a notion to come. Ain't been home in a while, so I thought I'd check on the old place."

"Well, it's still here. Look like it ain't goin nowhere." He paused. "What chu gon do with the house? Let it fall in?"

I sidestepped the critique and said, "Guess so. No need fixin it up. Ain't nobody gon live in it."

"Then let somebody tear it down. Just go 'head on and level it and be through with it."

I shrugged. "I don't know bout that. Not sure I can let it go yet."

Mr. John nodded and said, "It was mighty fine when yo granddaddy first built it. Mighty fine! Don't look like much now, but that was a hell of a house once upon a time."

"I'm sure it was."

"It was!" he declared as if I didn't believe it. "Abraham built that house pretty much by hisself. Didn't take him long neither!"

We paused.

"You come from good stock, boy. I'm tellin you! Yo folks

worked like mules. All of 'em. Couldn't nobody outpick yo momma in the cotton field. Nobody! Man or woman!"

I'd never heard that before. When I was growing up, people didn't talk about my mother.

"She was that good, Mr. John?"

"Sheit! Wunnit nobody better! Went up and down dem rows like a machine. Young, too. Couldn'ta been more'n fifteen or sixteen. But boy she could get it!"

I felt proud.

"All yo folks was like that. They wunnit but a generation removed from slavery, so they knowed how to work. We all did. But the Swintons was somethin else!"

"What really happened to my mother, Mr. John? Did you ever know?"

He took a deep breath and nodded. "Everybody knowed. We jes didn't talk about it."

"I wish somebody had. I've always wanted to know."

"You shoulda knowed. We shoulda told you. You and yo brother. But you know how we was then."

"Yessir, I know. But it's a new day now."

He nodded vigorously. "You right. You mighty right. I guess ain't nobody left to tell you but me."

He took a cigar from the front pocket of his overalls, lit it, and puffed slowly several times. I waited.

"She was a pretty girl, Jacob. Curvy and shapely—" he outlined the image with his hands "—like yo grandma had once been." He smiled through his memory. "You got her eyes, her nose, her smile."

That made me smile.

"Yo brother looked more like yo daddy. I saw him once in

town. He was a fine man, tall and thin, just wunnit worth a shit." He shrugged.

"Yo momma was jus tryin to get away from here. She didn't love him. She had mo sense than that."

"Why was she tryin to get away?"

His eyes narrowed. "Same reason everybody was, I guess. Hard life, hard livin."

I had so many questions but didn't know which ones to ask.

"Yo momma had a particularly hard time, Jacob. She wunnit like other girls."

"That's what Grandma said."

"Everybody knowed it. A blind man coulda seen that." He stared at me as if warning that this wasn't going to be easy. He then lowered the tailgate of his truck and wiggled upon it. I sat next to him.

"Yo momma was bout as bold as your granddaddy. They didn't see eye to eye. Folks said he beat her, but I don't know if that was true. Wouldn'ta shocked me if he did. We did that back then, when a child wouldn't mind, especially a girl, 'cause we feared she wouldn't be fit for marriage, and if she wunnit fit for marriage, she wunnit fit for nothin. So I guess yo granddaddy tried to straighten her out, but she wouldn't bend."

Mr. John stared into the distance, trying, it seemed, to soften what he knew would be a heavy blow.

"Grandma told me that," I said, "but was she really *that* bold?"

He chuckled. "You have no idea, boy. Yo momma was bout the bravest thang I ever seen." He paused then said, "And yo granddaddy meant to break her down."

"That's awful, Mr. John."

"I know, but that's how menfolks was. All of us. You seen it. You musta."

"I did. And I didn't like it."

"Well, wunnit nothin you could do about it. It was jes who we was."

I nodded, unsure of what more he might say, but certain I'd come too far not to hear it.

Mr. John smirked and added, "Yo momma got pregnant at fifteen. We didn't know whose it was. Didn't ask. She come to church one Sunday lookin pudgy round de stomach, so we knowed. We also knowed Abraham didn't like it. Not the fact that she was pregnant, but the fact that she wunnit married. Folks didn't believe in children born out of wedlock in those days. Sometimes they sent the girl away, other times they just dealt with it, but they never accepted it. Usually they made the girl stand before the church congregation and *beg pardon* as they called it. She'd be cryin and full of shame, but she'd do it."

"What about the boy? Did he have to do it, too?"

"Naw," he slurred. "We didn't have the same standard for boys and girls. It wunnit right, but folks thought girls oughta have more dignity since they carried the baby."

"That's wrong, Mr. John."

"I know it. But since most womenfolks agreed, that's what we did." He shrugged.

"So did she do it? Did she beg the pardon?"

"Didn't have no other choice. It's the only time I ever saw her tremble. That's when I knowed we was wrong. But I wunnit bold enough to say it."

He puffed on the cigar as he talked: "The preacher called her up and we all knew why. She knew this day was coming, too. It was just our way. So she stood with that unbreakable boldness and marched to the front of the church like she owned it. Folks whispered about her bein full o' herself, but I was glad she didn't crumble. The preacher said, 'You's a mighty fine young lady, Sarah Ann Swinton, who comes from a good family. But you done fell into sin, and the Lord ain't pleased.' A few murmured amen, but most of us bowed our heads and waited. 'We askin you, this morning, to confess your sin before God and be restored, that your bastard child might not bear the weight of your ungodliness.'"

"He called the baby a bastard?"

"Right there in that pulpit! Sho did! But that wunnit no surprise. That's how we thoughta kids born outta wedlock."

All I could do was shake my head.

"Still, Sarah Ann wunnit shame. She was nervous—I could see that. But she wunnit bout to break and cry in front of the church. I was proud of her for that. I just hate I didn't have the strength to stand with her."

Regret loomed large in his eyes.

"She stared at the congregation and said, 'I'm sorry if I embarrassed y'all. I didn't mean to. And I'm sorry if y'all ashamed of me. But I ain't ashamed of myself. Or my baby.' I'll never forget it. I always wondered where she'd got that strength from. Women said your grandma taught her behind Abraham's back. Musta been true. Folks' mouths fell open and some even called her blasphemous. But she didn't buckle. She just stood there, staring back at people who wanted her to degrade herself. But man, oh man, were they disappointed that day!"

I half smiled.

"That's what I think sent Abraham off the deep end. Not only that she was pregnant, which was bad enough, but that she wunnit sorry about it. She wouldn't bow to the laws of the church. She got up there, but she didn't disgrace herself. I think he saw her response as disrespectful to God, and he couldn't tolerate that. Not from one of his own. So he had to punish her somehow, *make* her sorry for what she'd done. It was a issue of honor."

"Honor?"

"That's probably what he thought. If she was unwilling to correct herself, somebody had to do it."

"That's terrible."

"Well, that ain't the worse part. Days later, they was fussin in the barn loft, folks said. I don't know what they was arguin bout, but according to what I heard, she tripped and fell from the loft to the ground below and lost the baby. Almost lost her life, too. Like to bled to death."

Mr. John saw the horror in my bulged eyes but kept right on talking.

"Some folks don't believe she fell. They think Abraham pushed her."

I gasped and held my breath.

"We come from all over the community that day when we heard the news. I was worried to death bout yo momma. We stood round in the yard like folks at a wake. Miss Liza, the healer, wouldn't let nobody in the house, includin yo grandma and granddaddy. Yo grandma was on the ground wailin, yo granddaddy was pacin the field, talkin out loud. Miss Liza worked on yo momma all night long. We heard her, inside the house, hummin and stompin and mumblin, till, just before day, she stepped out on the porch and said, 'Let her rest awhile. She'll be all right.' We shouted and lifted our hands as a bright sun chased the night away. Yo grandma had a fit, cryin and clappin in the spirit. Ain't never seen nobody rejoice like that. She woulda lost her mind if yo momma hada died that night."

Mr. John swayed side to side, causing the whole truck to tilt unsteadily.

"We looked around for Abraham, but couldn't find him. A few of us searched the woods, the riverbank, but seemed like he had disappeared. All day long we looked, but he wunnit nowhere to be found. Then, at evening, he showed up. Didn't look like hisself though. Looked like he had done seen the devil. Wouldn't say nothin to nobody. Stayed that way a week or better." Mr. John blew a long stream of cigar smoke into the air. "It was bad, son. Don't know what Abraham did in that barn, but I think he regretted it. Didn't never talk about it. Not far as I know."

"You think he pushed her, Mr. John?"

The old man cleared his throat and pondered awhile. "Mighta. Can't never tell." He fidgeted a bit, then looked at me sternly and said, "I think he did. Don't think he was tryin to kill her though. He was probably tryin to make her lose the baby. But he *almost* killed her. And that almost killed him."

I sucked my teeth to keep from cursing. I knew Granddaddy, and I knew what he'd been capable of.

"He loved her though, Jacob."

I frowned.

"We just did love different back then."

"Yessir. I know."

"Love didn't have nothin to do with feelins. It was hard work and sacrifice and makin sure chillen knew how to mind. Didn't have much to do with what you felt about 'em. Or what they felt about you."

"Don't I know."

"Abraham wunnit no different from the rest of us. We was poor, bitter people, son, who never knowed how to feel nothin. 'Cept pain. But sometimes you get tired of that, you know?"

"Yessir."

"What we wanted most was obedient chillen. And we meant to have it. Whatever the cost."

"Even the children's lives?"

"Yessiree! A disobedient child was the ruin of a people, we thought, so we didn't allow it. Plus, we needed someone beneath us, someone we could beat and low-grade—the way white folks had done us." He yelped. "A cryin shame is what it was."

I studied the nearby forest, wondering how many children had lived there and never felt loved.

"But anyway," he continued, "yo momma survived, but she wunnit never the same. Had a big pretty smile once, deep dimples in both cheeks, but after everything happened, she rarely smiled at all. Sometimes I'd speak to her and she'd look directly in my eyes without sayin a word. I knew she didn't mean no harm. It was just so sad seein her like that. It wunnit the way she'd always been.

"Girls liked yo momma. They wanted to be like her, but didn't have the courage. She was the spitting image of Abraham—inside *and* out. That's probably what made him so mad. She was a girl, and girls were supposed to obey and submit, but she wouldn't do it. It wunnit in her to do it.

"Men teased boys about who could handle Sarah Ann Swinton. Most of 'em didn't even try. Seemed like she didn't care nothin bout 'em. So she went about her business confident as any boy round here." He paused. "And you ain't never heard nobody read like Sarah Ann Swinton could read!"

"Really?"

He shook his head joyfully. "Listen to what I'm tellin you! When yo momma opened her mouth and read, the angels stood still!"

I chuckled at his exaggeration. Mr. John was nothing if not dramatic.

"I ain't lyin! Sarah Ann could reeead! She'd hold her head high and pronounce words like she owned 'em. I used to love when they'd ask her to read the morning scripture. Folks said amen even before she started." He clapped as he remembered. "Her voice was loud and light, like a church bell, and she always read slowly, saying each word thoroughly so you couldn't misunderstand it. I ain't explainin it right, but she could bring the house down! I'm tellin you!"

I thought of Rachel reading to you.

"Some folks didn't like it 'cause she was a girl, but some of us loved it. She just had a gift. That's all there was to it." He shrugged. "They say your grandma read to her at night. Don't know if that was true or not, but I guess it musta been. Sarah Ann had to get it from somewhere."

"Didn't she go to school?"

"Yeah, but no more'n any other child. Which wunnit much." He paused, then said, "She really was somethin else."

I tried to picture her in my mind, but I couldn't. "Nobody said much about her to me. Not even my own folks."

"I ain't surprised. You know how we was." He cleared his throat. "All that silence didn't do us no good though. It cost us more'n it protected us."

"You right about that."

He went on: "After the accident in the barn, I seen your momma the following Sunday morning, and she looked like a ghost. Everybody whispered about it, but nobody said nothin. She just stared forward like a crazy girl. Your grandma cried as she led her in and sat her down slowly. Abraham walked behind them, looking sad and pitiful, and took his place in the deacon's corner. I'll never forget the look in yo momma's eyes. Wasn't no spirit left in her. Just the shell of a girl who, seem like to me, came before her time."

The whole landscape around us shifted and swirled.

"I hate to tell you this, but you got a right to know. Yo mamma wunnit crazy. Or even wrong, from what I could tell. She was just—" he exhaled "—I don't know: too confident or brave or strong in a way menfolk didn't like. I don't know what you call it or what to make of it, but she come in the world different. Some kids is like that. They arrive with they own personality, and ain't nothin you can do about it—like it or not. We can beat 'em or try to make 'em change, but who they is is gon come out sooner or later. Simple as that." He tried to cackle but couldn't. "Your mother was one of 'em."

I chewed my thumbnail and kept listening.

"After seein her that Sunday morning, I come by the house later to check on her, and she was sittin in the livin room, rockin like folks what done lost they mind. Yo grandpa was out in the shed somewhere, and when I found him, he asked me if I needed somethin, and I told him I was just checkin on the family since Sarah Ann looked so bad that morning, but he told me to mind my own business. Said she was fine. At least she would be. So I left.

"I almost asked about the baby, but I didn't. I knowed she had done lost it." He touched my shoulder heavily. "I'm just tellin you 'cause you asked. And 'cause you oughta know."

I sniffled a little, I think, as nature sang me a lullaby.

"She was tall, black, and pretty. Then, after everything happened, she never did get back right. Got a little better over time though. Started smilin a little every now and then, but never did read out loud no more. I don't think they asked her to. I still hear her voice in my head sometimes."

He stopped for a while, then said, "Of course she married that fella from Plumerville, and moved down there. Don't know why he killed her, but I can probly guess. Same reason yo granddaddy did what he did."

When our eyes met, Mr. John patted my thigh lightly and said, "Ain't nothin to do now but accept it and keep on livin. Knowin the truth oughta help us do better. It *oughta*."

Minutes passed, it seemed, as Mr. John put out the cigar and broke off a wad of tobacco and began gnawing it slowly. He seemed to be waiting for me to speak, but I had nothing to say. So I lit a cigarette and dragged on it till my nerves settled.

"I wish I'd known her."

"I know you do. But it wunnit meant to be. You mighta done better; mighta not've. Can't never tell."

A hawk lifted from a nearby tree and glided through the clear blue sky.

"Anyway, glad to see you today. Always good when a man comes home."

"Yessir. Glad to be here."

Mr. John spit tobacco juice on the dry, dusty road.

"I 'preciate you checkin on the place. That's mighty nice o' you."

"Oh, it ain't nothin. What else I gotta do?"

He hopped down from the tailgate, so I did the same.

We spoke of other things—lighter, easier, more manageable things—then shook hands before he drove away. I leaned upon my car, thinking about my mother. I didn't want to believe any of what Mr. John had said, but I knew it was true.

I walked slowly across the field. I realized I didn't have to forgive Granddaddy. Just because he'd been my grandfather and had done right by Esau and me, I wasn't obligated to forgive him. Maybe I never will.

Still, I was glad to be home. I walked for hours, touching trees, weeds, and leaves, which normally I'd taken for granted. Not since before leaving Arkansas for good had I spent so much personal time on the land. You and I had surveyed it, all those years ago, but I was conscious of your presence in a way that limited my freedom. This is not to say you were a bother or anything, but rather to admit that being there alone allowed me to lower my guard and mill about freely.

The day warmed as I relived the confrontation between

Granddaddy and my mother. I couldn't get the image out of my mind. Then I thought of how I'd treated you. I remembered the day your mother called the police because I'd hit you, and suddenly my anger with Granddaddy eased. I'd thought I was teaching you a vital life lesson. I'm sure he thought the same. Still, I couldn't believe I'd done anything as awful as he'd done. But perhaps I had. If you'd told your story, I would've looked like the same monster I thought he was. That's how I knew, finally, how terrible I'd been. I couldn't face you any more than he could've faced me.

The more I thought about my mother, the more I adored her. Truth is, I married her. Rachel's bold, assertive nature had excited me at first. It convinced me she'd raise good children and maintain a household whether she liked it or not. I certainly wouldn't have liked a woman with a bowed-down head. This sounds contradictory, but it's true. I'd wanted someone self-assured who *chose* to submit because she believed in me. Grandma wasn't quite so daring, and now I see why. But I must admit that, as a child, I didn't admire her sweet surrender. I thought of her as weak sometimes, quite honestly, and I pitied her. I'd wanted her to confront Granddaddy on a few occasions, to give him a good run for his effort, but she never did. I see now that had she done so, it might've cost her life.

No one should diminish themselves to prove their love.

I've kept the house in Kansas City. It's yours. My greatest hope is that you'll return one day and find love here. Your mother and I planted it carefully, amidst everything else, and it's still waiting for you. Believe me. It's here. I went home one day, too.

FEBRUARY 1ST, 2004

I had to take a break. I'm sicker each day now, more drained than the day before. My energy is practically gone, but there are a few more things I need to say.

I stayed over that night at a hotel in Morrilton, just as you and I had done years ago. At daybreak, I went back to the old home place, just to say goodbye, but I couldn't leave. Something troubled my mind, begging me to remember what I'd apparently forgotten.

"Love you, Momma!" I whispered, then covered my mouth. "I'm sorry about what happened to you." A cool breeze tickled the grass. "You have a grandson named Isaac. And he's brilliant just like you." Then, out of nowhere, as if someone had borrowed my tongue, I said, "Granddaddy was wrong. But he didn't hate you. He raised us 'cause he loved you."

It felt good to speak to her. I remembered what Grandma used to say all the time: *you'll understand it better by and by.* And, finally, I did.

I went to town, straight to McGee Monument Company. The guy running the place, Bart McGee, was the grandson of the founder. I saw their pictures on the wall. He was kind and very sensitive to my needs.

"I'm looking for two headstones," I said. "One for my mother, the other for my brother."

"Sure. We're glad to help." He was white, but he was excited to serve me. Or he needed my money badly.

"What exactly are you looking for?"

"I'm not sure. Just something nice to put on their graves."

"Okay. Do you want a flat stone or something upright?"

"Upright."

"Okay. I see. They're a little more expensive, but they're more elegant, too. Let me show you a few options."

He led the way to a wide-open space in the rear of the store, filled with grave markers of every conceivable style. Some were shaped like butterflies, others like trees and crucifixes. I liked the ones shaped like hearts. But when he told me the price, I shuddered.

"Yeah, they can be pretty costly, but they last forever."

"I can't afford that. But it's what I want."

"I understand. The more reasonable ones are the ones we don't have to stylize. They're just as nice."

I looked around awhile longer and settled for two identical light gray marble uprights. I could've saved money and bought a double stone, but since Momma and Esau were not buried side by side, I wanted the markers directly above where each lay. I knew Esau's resting place; I'd ask Mr. John about Momma's.

The guy led me into a small office. "What would you like written on them?" He took a seat behind a desk much too large for the room. "The name and date engraving are included in the price. We'll add any short phrase if you like, free of charge."

"I haven't thought about that."

"Well, now's the time," he smiled and handed me a notepad and pencil. "No rush. Remember, it's forever."

I sighed and reclined in a chair opposite his desk and wrote,

Esau Swinton
1939–1956
"My dear brother"

I frowned. It felt wrong. I tried "loving brother and son" but I didn't like that either, so I scratched it out. My last attempt, "Angel of Heaven," I liked least, so I tore the sheet from the pad and crumpled it into a ball.

"This is hard, man!" I said and stood to pace a bit.

He smiled coolly. "I understand. It's perfectly fine to take your time. Sometimes people take weeks to decide."

"But I don't have that kind of time. I'm leaving today."

He nodded and repeated. "I understand. You don't have to add anything if you don't want to. It's just an option."

"I do want to! I have to say something."

"Then you have to decide. I can't help you with that. You can look at examples on other stones if you like."

I shook my head. "I want to write something myself."

"Of course."

I returned to the chair.

"Were you all very close?"

"Yessir. Sort of."

He nodded. "Perhaps simply say what you wish for them. That comforts the heart sometimes."

I thought about that, then wrote, "Rest in the Arms of God." It was okay, but still I wasn't satisfied. Then something came to me. I wrote it as neatly as possible:

"Your love was enough."

That was it. That was what I wanted to say to my brother.

"You got it?"

"One of them. Now for the other."

I'd thought a phrase for Momma would be easier, but it wasn't. I hadn't known her the way I'd known Esau, so I couldn't think of anything to say. "Rest in Peace" was too common and impersonal, and "Loving Mother" didn't say what she'd been to me. I had no idea choosing a tombstone could be so difficult.

I went to the showroom and read all kinds of phrases on headstones, some of which were beautiful, but too much. A frail old black man, whom I hadn't noticed, touched my back and said, "Sorry for your loss." I turned and said, "Thank you." He leaned upon a walking cane as if he might, at any moment, fall over.

"Who'd you lose?" he asked freely.

"My mother. I'm trying to decide what to put on her gravestone."

"I done buried my mother, father, sisters, brothers, wife, and now my son. I done outlived damn near everybody." He chuckled sadly. "It ain't a blessin." His eyes were yellowed and weary. "I don't guess folks really mind what you say on their graves. Anything sincere'll work."

"You just lost your son, sir?"

"Week ago."

"I'm so sorry."

"Yep. My only boy. Got two girls left."

"How did he pass?"

"Don't know really. They say heart attack, but I don't believe that."

"No? Why not?"

"He wunnit no size! Thin as a bird. Always has been. Can't see why his heart woulda gave out. Of all the deaths, my boy's is the hardest." His eyes narrowed as he squeezed the cane intensely.

I touched his shoulder, and said again, "I'm so sorry, sir."

"It's all right, it's all right," he murmured and relaxed a bit. "God gon do what God wants to. Lawd knows that's true."

"Are you gonna put something on his headstone? Something other than his name and dates?"

"I believe I will."

I waited.

"I think I want it to say *The Only Begotten Son*. That's what I think."

"That'll be nice."

"Yeah. Hope so. Well, you take care and put somethin nice on yo momma's stone."

"Yessir. I'll try."

He hobbled away, and I prayed he'd find peace. People say God knows how much we can bear, but sometimes I'm not so sure.

Back in the man's office, I wrote on the pad:

Sarah Ann Swinton
1920–1943
"Your Courage Will Never Be Forgotten"

That's the best I could do. It's what I meant in my heart, what I wanted her to know. I wasn't sure about the dates. I'd have to ask Mr. John about that. But I handed the man the notepad anyway. He smiled and said, "Beautiful. Just beautiful. They'll be happy for this."

He calculated the total, I paid him practically every dollar I had. I'd put aside enough for gas, but nothing more. I didn't need anything more.

FEBRUARY 3RD, 2004

I left the monument store feeling good. This was something I'd always wanted to do. Guilt melted away as I drove to Mr. John's, wondering if, in fact, the dead really see us. If so, I hoped Momma and Esau were happy. Grandma and Grand-daddy, too, for that matter.

Mr. John was sitting on his porch, cracking pecans. He wore the same overalls he always wore and a straw hat that had seen better days.

"Whatchasay there!" he shouted. "Thought you was long gone by now."

"Yessir. Thought I would be, too. But I decided to do something I should've done years ago."

"What's that?"

I took a seat in a worn rocker next to him. "Put a head-stone on Esau's and Momma's graves."

"Oh yessuh! Now that's really somethin! Mighty fine. Mighty fine!"

"I shoulda done it a long time ago."

"You doin it now. That's what matters. A man shouldn't chastise himself when he's trying to do better."

I sighed. "Thank you, Mr. John."

He nodded and offered fresh-shelled pecan halves, but I shook my head.

"I came by to ask you something."

"All righty. Hope I can help."

"I was trying to confirm when my mother was born. I know it was around '20 or '21 'cause Grandma said Momma was eighteen or nineteen when Esau was born, but I wanted to get it right for the tombstone. Thought you might know."

Mr. John swallowed a handful of pecans as he thought, then hollered, "Ernestine! Come out here for a minute."

She came to the screen, fussing, "Whatchu want, man? I'm tryin to—" until she saw me and exclaimed, "Well, lookie here! If it ain't ole Jacob Swinton, looking like yo grandpa!"

We hugged, and I asked if she'd baked a cake lately.

"Got a ole pound cake in there I made yesterday. Might be fit to eat." She winked. "I'll bring you a piece *and* wrap you one to take with you. How bout that?"

"Yes, ma'am!"

"You can bring me a piece, too," Mr. John teased.

"I ain't bringin you nothin! Last thing you need is another piece o' cake while you sittin round here eatin them greasy-ass pecans all mornin!"

He looked at me and shook his head. I laughed. They had bantered like this since I knew them.

"Listen, woman," he said, shifting the mood, "wasn't Sarah Ann born the same year as Ethel May?"

"Whatchu askin that for?"

"'Cause Jacob tryin to find out when his momma was born so he can put it on her tombstone."

"Oh, oh, oh! Okay… Let me see." She closed her eyes and pursed her lips. "Naw, she was born the next spring. Ethel May come in November of '20, Sarah Ann come in April of '21."

Mr. John frowned. "You sho? Seem like to me Sarah Ann come before Ethel May?"

"Naw she didn't! Ethel May come first. Sarah Ann come just after the flood. I remember it well."

Ethel May was their daughter who died of polio at age seven. I'd heard of her, and I'd also heard of the flood of 1920, how the river rose like morning mist, swallowing everything in its path. Everyone's farm was destroyed and lots of houses washed away. Plenty folks drowned, too. Only house worth keeping, folks said, was Abraham Swinton's. I'd heard the story a thousand times. He'd built it himself, upon cinderblocks, having anticipated such a disaster. People shook their heads when they told this story, as if having beheld the workings of a master craftsman.

"So Sarah Ann come in '21?" Mr. John repeated.

"That's right. April of '21."

I nodded and thanked them for the information. "Do you remember exactly when she died?"

Miss Ernestine closed her eyes again, but shook her head. "Naw, I don't 'member that. It was cold though. First time I saw you and yo brother y'all was bundled up in raggedy coats and hats. Now I 'member *that*!"

"'Stine!"

"It's true! Ain't no shame in it! They was handsome boys! All bright-eyed and eager-lookin."

I smiled. "Grandma said that, when Momma died, I was walkin, but not talkin too good, so she had to be in her early twenties, I guess."

"That's right," Mr. John confirmed. "She wunnit no more'n twenty-two or twenty-three at the most."

"She was probly round bout twenty-two, I guess," Miss Ernestine offered.

I used their phone to call Bart McGee and confirm the dates: 1921–1943. Miss Ernestine brought me a piece of lemon pound cake on a sheet of paper towel, and I gorged it down in two bites.

"Don't hurt yourself, boy!" Mr. John teased playfully.

We chatted the afternoon away. Then, around three, I said, "I need one more favor, sir. Can you show me where my momma is buried? I wanna put the stone right over her grave."

We hopped into his battered little pickup truck and made our way to the cemetery. We parked in the weeded lane and got out.

"She's right over there," he pointed and led the way to the general area where the Swintons lay. "Right here," he said when we arrived. "Right next to yo grandma."

I was a bit surprised. "I thought she mighta been over there, closer to Esau."

"Naw, she right here. I remember it well. That tree was to

my left, and it blocked the wind pretty good that day. Man, it was cold!"

"Was it *that* cold?"

"Freezin! I bet it was damn near zero. Couldn't hardly dig the grave, the ground was so hard."

He spit a mouthful of tobacco juice to the side. "Guess you know where yo brother is." He nodded toward the base of another tree.

"Yessir. I'll never forget that."

"This a good thing you doin. Mighty good thing. Gon mean somethin to somebody one day. You mark my word."

"Hope so."

We looked around awhile, perusing graves, talking about people and natural disasters, until the headstone truck arrived.

Suddenly, something tingled just beneath my skin. Mr. John noticed.

"It's all right, son. This what they been waitin for."

The truck backed as close as it could get to the graves, then two white men carried the slabs of marble and set them where we directed. The monuments looked awkward and out of place at first, since the other graves bore only small, flat metal plates, but I didn't fret. I'd done what I'd promised.

When the white men left, Mr. John said, "Yo people is pleased. They know. They here right now. Especially yo momma and brother. They see you. And they thank you for not forgettin 'em. We all do."

My throat closed. I couldn't say a word.

"I'll be in the truck. Take you a minute wit 'em. Ain't no rush." He touched my arm lightly and limped away.

I read the inscriptions twenty times before saying, "I hope

you like it. It's the best I could do. I'll be back soon. Love you both," and touched the face of each stone as if caressing the very flesh of my people.

By 5:30, I was on I-40, headed back to Kansas City.

I'm telling you this because I did it for you. You'll want to know these people one day—where they lay, how they fit into your story. When you get to the graveyard, you won't have to search hard for them. Their spirits—and these stones—will greet you.

Just remember that, although we were flawed, we were marvelous, too.

FEBRUARY 5TH, 2004

When I returned home, peace settled all around me. I wasn't burdened the way I'd once been. I understood, finally, that blood ties people biologically, but not emotionally. Our hearts were strangers. Still, I longed for you, thought of you every day, wished you'd call, but finally accepted that you probably wouldn't. There was nothing you needed from me anymore.

I started life over again. I was almost sixty. I had lost fifty pounds smoking instead of eating. People didn't recognize me. A few of the fellas asked about my health, and I said I was fine. They knew I was lying. Bobby Joe came by one morning and knocked, and I never opened the door. I couldn't let him see me that way.

To be honest, I've been dying a long time. For ten years, all I did was work, smoke, read, and listen to music. I hope your generation has musicians equal to ours. I don't know how anyone survives without them.

It's not been a horrible life, Isaac. It's just been a lonely one. But that was my own doing. Reading taught me that a man's life is his own responsibility, his own creation. Blaming others is a waste of time. No one can make you happy if you're determined to be miserable. And, for many years, I was.

Then, one morning, I woke with the sudden urge to see you. I think I had decided to die. I was calm and coolheaded. All I wanted was to look you in the face and tell you *I'm sorry*. I had wounded you beyond my capacity to heal you.

If you get nothing else from this letter, understand that I never knew how to love. I dreamed of it, but I never experienced it. What I knew was pain. So that's what I gave you. I'd never seen a black life free from it, so my job as a father, I assumed, was to prepare your back for the load. I hope that, after you read this, you'll return my pain to me. But you might not. We get used to it, the weight of pain, and when it threatens to go, we sometimes hold on to it for dear life. But there's no joy while it lingers near.

Perhaps you'll have a child one day, biological or otherwise, and you'll see how easy it is to hurt the one you love. A man believes that, when he becomes a father, he'll love perfectly. But this isn't true. Love doesn't make us perfect; it makes us *want to be*. By the time you discover this, your imperfections have done their damage.

I should tell you that I started driving to Chicago that morning. I knew your address because you'd written it on documents when your mother died. I assumed you hadn't moved. I just wanted to see you, to make sure you were okay. Well, that's not the whole truth. Really, I wanted us to be together again. To act like a father and son should. I wanted to say things to you, face-to-face. But the longer I drove, the more convinced I became that you wouldn't welcome me or want to see me, so I turned around and came home. I made it as far as Columbia, Missouri, I think. Maybe a little farther. I pulled into a gas station off I-70, and sat for hours. It couldn't've worked. There were too many hurdles for you to get over. All I heard in my head was what you had said to your mother a few nights before her funeral: *I have my own life to live. Dad has his.*

I got out of the car, leaned upon the hood, and smoked cigarettes as cars and 18-wheelers zoomed by.

I never made it to you. But I started coming.

FEBRUARY 7TH, 2004

When, that evening, I reentered the house, I sat in your mother's reading chair and agonized over what I'd done. I heard her say, *You should've gone. He doesn't hate you.*

I responded aloud: "It doesn't matter now. I didn't go."

You can always go again.

"No, I can't. I'm done tryin. It's too much."

What if he cries when he sees you and says how badly he's needed you?

"What if he doesn't?"

What would you regret most in the end? Not going? Or going and being rejected?

It was the latter for me. So I sighed, drew a bath, and soaked as Muddy Waters's coarse growling dulled my misery. Midway through the cleansing, my breathing became labored. I wasn't very alarmed at first, but in the coming weeks, I knew something was wrong. On the phone, my doctor told me, as I explained my symptoms, that I needed to get to a hospital immediately. *Waiting could kill you*, he said.

The idea of living longer didn't excite me. In fact, it translated into more days of sadness. But I suppose it wasn't my time, as Grandma would've said. So I panted and wheezed for another month before, finally, dragging myself to an emergency room.

The doctor examined my condition, then scolded me. Had I come sooner, he said, the news might've been better. I shrugged. He didn't understand my situation; he didn't know my story.

"You've got a mass on your lungs, Mr. Swinton, the size of a baseball."

I nodded slowly, refusing to look at him.

"There's really not much we can do now. If only you had—"

"Can I go?"

He blinked, confused. "Excuse me?"

"Home. Can I go?"

He frowned. "We need to discuss treatment options, sir. This is a very serious matter. You can't live like this. Nothing is guaranteed, of course, but new trial medicines have proven quite promising, especially in buying you a little more—"

"I don't want it."

"But you haven't heard—"

"I said, I don't want it."

He got the point, finally. "Very well. Suit yourself. But I have to tell you that this is not wise. And, at some point, the pain will become unbearable."

"It already has."

He was obviously disappointed. "Do you understand that soon I'll be unable to help you? There'll be no relief for you."

"There's none now."

He stared, perplexed. I refused to elaborate. I just wanted to go home.

"You can barely breathe, Mr. Swinton."

"I know."

"Anything is worth a try, don't you think?"

"No sir, I don't."

He yielded. "Fine. Have it your way. You know how to reach me." With that, he stood and exited the sterile white room. Thinking he might return, I sat and waited, only to realize he really had surrendered. So I buttoned my shirt, hopped off the exam table, and walked out, looking over my shoulder as if the doctor might run after me, compelling me, once again, to reconsider. He didn't.

I thought that, although you hadn't ever called me, you might come if you heard I was dying, but I didn't mean to meet you on my back. Down home, when a man fell *low sick*, as we said, most avoided him altogether. They'd go by and ask after him, but they wouldn't behold him on his sick bed. That was disrespectful. When he recovered, folks would boast of his endurance, his tenacity, but they wouldn't speak of his weakened state. If he died, they'd boast all the same and remember him as one who gave Death *a hell of a run*. That's the phrase they used. But since I assumed you didn't know that phrase, for the maintenance of a man's dignity, I refused to let you see me at my worst. I had no confidence that you would, as the song says, *look beyond my faults and see my needs.*

When I got home from the hospital, I listened to "Stood

on the Banks of Jordan" for the umpteenth time and stared through the living room window. Death sat next to me, holding my hand. She was, once again, draped in flowing blue, with an Afro and dangling gold earrings. *There's no rush*, she said. *I've only come to show you the way, to accompany you when you're ready.* No man knows when he shall die, Isaac, but he knows when he's ready.

I was almost ready.

FEBRUARY 8TH, 2004

I didn't go back to the doctor until the Monday after my sixty-first birthday. My breathing had become so labored I had no choice. Several days at work I almost passed out, so, after the doctor gave me the bad news, I told Charlie and the boys I'd had enough, and clocked out for the last time. Officially, I retired from the post office after forty years of service, but they knew better. They couldn't even look at me as I walked away.

One Sunday morning, months after I'd left work for good, Charlie stopped by to check on me. He did this occasionally, and I appreciated him for it. Otherwise, I would've had no visitors at all.

He knew I was dying. Sorrow and pity glazed his eyes. He would never say it, but he knew. He gave me the dignity of acting normal so I wouldn't feel sad or embarrassed. That's how men loved each other in my day. He came in and sat on the end of the sofa before I could offer him a seat.

"What's wrong?" I asked.

He shook his head slowly, like one trying to understand a difficult thing. That's when I got really concerned.

"It's Charlie Junior," he said. "Somebody hurt him."

"Hurt him? What do you mean?"

"They found him last night, bloody and bruised, on the side of the road."

I struggled to sit up. "What! What are you talking about?"

He shrugged and sighed. "Kayla said he didn't come home last night, so she got worried and called the police."

"Charlie!"

"Yeah." He blinked as if returning from a trance. "Doctors said he'll be all right, but he was beat up pretty bad."

I'd known Charlie Junior since he was a toddler. You remember me boasting of him, I'm sure, of his strong athletic abilities. He was a hell of a quarterback, drafted to Auburn on full scholarship, then, a few years later, to the Dallas Cowboys. Charlie never tired of telling us about him. He was slightly younger than you, but he was certainly a father's dream.

Now, sitting in my living room confused, I couldn't figure out what had happened to him.

I kept shaking my head. "This don't make no sense!"

Charlie appeared delirious. "I know, I know."

"Did they rob him?"

"They're looking into that. His wife said his face was covered with blood. Bruises all over his body. But no cuts or gunshot wounds."

I didn't know what else to say, so I repeated, "It's gotta be a robbery or something."

"That's what I thought, but his wallet was still on him. It had a couple hundred dollars in it. Why didn't they take that?"

What could I say? "He's gonna be fine, Charlie. He's a strong boy! He'll pull through."

Charlie tried to smile, but couldn't. I touched his right shoulder—I certainly didn't hug him—and told him to keep the faith. He stood and paced a bit, then sighed and sat in your mother's reading chair.

"I don't understand it, Jacob. Somethin ain't right."

"What are you thinkin?"

"I don't know. It just don't add up. Who woulda done something like this to my boy?"

I repeated my suspicion of robbery, but he said, "Naw, man. That ain't it. I'm telling you, that ain't it."

"How you know?"

"'Cause they didn't rob him! They didn't take nothin he had!" Charlie frowned. "It's something else. Something we don't know nothin bout."

Hard as I tried, I couldn't think of anything else it could be.

"I asked Kayla if he might be having an affair, and she said no. She didn't sense anything like that, so..." He shrugged.

"Maybe some white boys did it, you know? Successful black NFL player and all."

He started pacing again. "I don't know."

I murmured, "We just gotta pray—"

"I don't wanna pray!" he shouted. "I wanna know what happened to my boy!"

"I know you do, Charlie, but take it easy. Everything's gon be all right."

Charlie stood at the glass storm door, staring into a silent world.

"Sit down, man. You makin me nervous."

He returned to the chair. "I'm sorry, Jacob. I just feel so helpless."

"I know you do." We stared in opposite directions.

"We drivin down tomorrow evening."

"Oh, that's good. You can see him for yoself."

Charlie was thinking something he wasn't saying, but I couldn't get it out of him. "Let me know if I can do anything."

"Just take care of yoself," he said and rose. "I'ma get on back to the house in case Kayla calls."

A week later, he returned, more troubled than before. After letting him in, I resumed my place on the sofa and, once again, he took your mother's chair. His eyes shifted wildly.

"What happened, Charlie?"

He shook his head. "I can't understand it, man. You raise a child, thinkin you know him, then you discover you don't know him at all."

"What are you talkin about?"

His head dropped like a heavy stone. "Didn't nobody rob him, Jacob. Somebody beat him up, but they didn't rob him."

"What was it, then?"

He studied the floor awhile, then looked at me sadly. "It was a hate crime, they said. Somebody wrote *faggot* on his windshield."

Charlie said the word with venom and pain so harsh I practically shuddered.

"What? What do you mean, man? You ain't makin sense!"

He sighed as if taking his final breath: "When the police found him, they saw the word written in red lipstick on Junior's glass. They don't know who wrote it, but Kayla found out."

"How'd she find out?"

"She went through his pockets at the hospital. Found a scrap piece o' paper with a man's name and number on it. So she called him."

I definitely didn't want to hear this part, but Charlie volunteered: "The man told her he loved my boy, Jacob." Charlie shook his head, unable to believe his own words. "That's what she said he said. They been messin around a little over a year. Fell out about somethin."

"Charlie."

"I know. It don't make no sense to me either."

"Well, did you ask Junior about it? You said he regained consciousness, right?"

He looked at me again, this time with fire in his eyes. "Yeah, I asked him about it. And he lied."

"Lied?"

"Yea. Told me he knew the guy, but wunnit nothin happenin between them."

"Why you say he lyin?"

"'Cause I know my son. I can tell when he's lyin. Always could. I didn't press him in the hospital, but I knew."

Charlie's slow, calculated nodding made me nervous.

"Jesus, man. That's...so...crazy."

I know I should've told him about you, should've confessed that, as fathers, we were in the same boat, and perhaps we could've been honest, completely honest, for the first time in our lives. But, instead, I covered his shame with silence. I was embarrassed for him, so I didn't do the right thing.

Charlie left, and we never spoke of the incident again.

Charlie Junior and Kayla stayed together though. They had a baby a few months later, a little boy named Charlie III, who they called Trey. The boy looks just like his daddy. Charlie showed me a picture. I was too jealous to be happy.

If I could go back in time, I'd tell Charlie the truth and urge him to love his boy regardless. I'd tell him that every man chooses his own life, and that a parent's job is to respect that choice. I might even tell him how I drove you away by wanting you to be something you weren't.

Now that I need you, I don't care what you are. Even if I weren't dying, I'd still need you. A man's son is his truth unadorned. When he can look at him and be proud, his fatherhood is complete. Mine never will be. I can't look at you now. And my pride in you is still in progress, although I've come a mighty long way. God will have to take me the rest of the journey.

Perhaps you're a famous painter in Chicago. If you are, hopefully, you've rendered your mother on canvas. No one could capture her beauty, her elegance, better than you, so if you haven't done this, get busy doing it. The world needs that kind of splendor on display.

Last night, I lifted myself from the sofa with every ounce of strength I could muster, and fell to my knees and cried out, *I'm sorry, Isaac.* You weren't there, but you were there—standing before me, disbelieving that this day had come. You were the father and I the son because I needed your grace, your forgiveness. Your mother had said it would come to this.

FEBRUARY 10TH, 2004

I can see the Old Ship of Zion now, easing across the water, coming quietly for me. You are in the prime of your life, loving some man freely, I suppose, but yourself mostly, I pray. If not, start doing it. *Time waits for no man*, Granddaddy used to say. And this is true.

When you read this, I'll be in the next world. Don't cry for me, son. I've cried enough for myself. And have no regrets about us. There is nothing for which you are to blame, unless you've now made your own mistakes and hurt others, which you may have. Every man has. But most of those hurts—at least many of them—are blooms of seeds I planted in you. You must learn to uproot unwanted seeds without destroying the entire harvest. This is the son's lesson. Nurture good sprouts, Isaac. Toss weeds aside and never think of them again. Just remember that sprouts and weeds are planted together, and weeds have a valuable function. They teach you what to avoid, what not to embrace. There is no good planting without them.

All I think of now is you. This means I love you. I feel it in my heart—that sense that nothing and no one else matters. I've always wanted to know that feeling, and now I do. The sad thing is that you won't hear me say *I'm sorry*. But I did say it. Perhaps in this letter you'll feel it, hear it in my tone, and let my words love you better than I ever did.

Just one last request: tell people I tried. If there is a funeral, and if you attend it, please tell them I tried. You are free to say I failed, too, for, in so many ways, that is the gospel truth, but at least say I tried. Recall, if you will, the few joys we shared—you, your mother, and I—and tell them I left you the house although you didn't want it. Tell them about our trip to the land, how you loved it and later painted it more beautifully than I had remembered. Tell them you graduated from college debt-free because I paid the tuition. Tell them I wasn't always a good father, but I was always a man.

And, if at all possible, take me home. Whether in a casket or a vase, please take me home. Don't leave me in Kansas City. Honeysuckles don't bloom here in springtime. Neighbors don't drop by if they haven't seen you in a while. This is not my home. I can't stay here. Lay me next to my brother, beneath the little tree in the cemetery. I'll have peace then. If what black people say is true, I'll meet Esau again and never long for this world. I'll meet my mother, too, and, hopefully, she'll love me the way your mother loved you. I'll confront Granddaddy about what he did and maybe he'll apologize, and we'll all be happy in eternity. I'll tell Grandma that her

dream came true: her great-grandson got a college education. But she probably already knows.

This is all I have to say. If this isn't enough, I have nothing
else to give. I would give you my life, but it's already spent.
The most precious thing I leave you is the land. It's yours.
Never sell it. It will support you when the world casts you
aside. If you end up like me, with nothing and no one, you
can always return to it, and it will love you and sustain you
without judgment. If you don't think you want it, keep it
anyway. It may be all you have one day.

Finally, I leave you this charge: Live your life freely, Isaac.
Rise above our history and be your unapologetic self. Just remember that I meant well. Even in my failure, I truly meant
well.

Your Father,
Jacob

★ ★ ★ ★ ★

To those who read this book in manuscript form and affirmed its worth:

Joyce White, Kyle Fox, LaNiece Littleton, Joan Littleton,
Obata Kufanya Tena, Nkiruka Kufanya Tena,
Rodney Goode, William DuBose, Lisa Black-Noel,
Rose Norment, D. Channsin Berry,
Georgene Bess-Montgomery, and Jericho Brown.